A NOVELIZATION BY DAVID LEVITHAN
ORIGINAL STORY BY MARC HYMAN & JON ZACK

New York   London   Toronto   Sydney   Singapore

First Simon Spotlight edition January 2004
Copyright © 2004 by Paramount Pictures

SIMON SPOTLIGHT
An imprint of Simon & Schuster
Children's Publishing Division
1230 Avenue of the Americas
New York, NY 10020

Designed by Ann Sullivan
The text of this book was set in AGaramond.

Printed in the United States of America
10 9 8 7 6 5 4 3 2 1

Library of Congress Control Number 2003106084

ISBN 0-689-86481-7

① Kyle

STUDENT I.D. #12215509
GPA 3.1
CLASS RANK 105/281
First S.A.T. score: ?

Have you ever had something you wanted? Something just out of reach? Something that would change your life forever?

What if you had the chance to grab it, but risked losing it at the same time?

What would you do?

Looking back, I wouldn't change a thing. You do what you think you have to do at the time. Sometimes because you're curious. Sometimes because you're desperate.

Sometimes because you're seventeen.

I am not the only one who's been through this. I know that. I am just one of the few who tried to do something about it.

You go through your life being told you can do anything. When you're a kid, it's okay to want to be a firefighter, a rock star, the president of the United States, and an astronaut—all at the same time. If you're lucky, you make it through elementary school without being tracked, categorized, slotted, and prepackaged. But then grades start to matter. The future starts to loom. And everyone—everyone—starts to talk about the S.A.T.

Last year the S.A.T. was administered to nearly two million students. An admission requirement of 90 percent of all colleges and universities. Scores range from 500 to 1600 for the standardized test.

Standardized, meaning a kid is a kid is a kid is a kid. Justice is supposed to be blind, and the S.A.T. is supposed to be blinder. It's not supposed to matter whether you're a preppy rich kid or a girl in the projects or a farm boy in the middle of nowhere or a pregnant girl in suburbia. The S.A.T. isn't supposed to favor anybody.

But we all know that's bullshit.

The preppy rich kid's parents will spend one thousand dollars on an S.A.T. tutor for their son. The girl in the projects will get a word problem about counting livestock. The farm boy in the middle of nowhere won't have access to the prep guides that any suburban high school has by the dozen. The pregnant girl will, quite frankly, have other things to worry about.

This is how our future is mapped out.

It's all part of the drill these days. Stanford 9s, CATs, ITBS, Woodcock-Johnson. A blur of standardized tests whose results put me in my place:

Average.

But the S.A.T. is different. Because while the other exams try to define who you are, the S.A.T. defines who you'll be.

Try to get into a great college with an average score.

It's not going to happen.

Try to reach for your dream job without going to a great college.

It's going to be much, much harder.

All because of one test.

So I got a job to pay for all the prep courses. I worked stacking packages in a postal warehouse. Hours and hours of lifting—heavy lifting. All to raise my score. All so I could play the game like the rich kids do. For every hundred boxes I carried, I learned ten word problems.

I learned the gimmicks. How less is more. How wrong can be right. How it's not about learning.

"You all have to use the tricks," the instructor told us, underlining the words "PLUGGING

IN" on his knock-off blackboard. "It's not about what you know. It's about how well you take the test."

I gave it the old college try. I studied until I was a zombie. I worked the "tricks" like they were the meaning of life.

And I scored a 1320. Not enough.

I cancelled those scores and tried again.

1250.

Cancelled.

And again.

1140.

Cancelled.

Getting those scores was like having someone rip up my future right in front of me.

There were places I wanted to go. I've known for a very long time what I want to do with my life. Maybe it started the first time I turned a scattering of wooden blocks into a building. Or the first time I drew two walls, a floor, and a roof with my crayons. I loved designing. I loved the act of creation, the thought that you can turn lines and patterns from your mind into something real, something you can build and that will be able to stand forever. I wanted to be an architect. No—more than that. I wanted to be a great architect. And for me that meant going to Cornell University. The best of the best.

But none of that mattered to Cornell if I didn't get a decent score.

None of it.

There was someone I wanted to be. Not just an architect. But someone who mattered. Someone who had a grip on his life.

Not like my brother Larry. Still living at home, in his mid-twenties. Still partying hard and living light.

When I got home, I saw an envelope waiting for me on my drafting table. My mother, an elementary school teacher, had put one of her gold stars on it. But she hadn't opened it.

It was my latest round of S.A.T. scores.

My latest chance at a future.

I took out my Cornell letter-opener. I looked to my wall to see the goal I'd posted up there, the score I'd need for Cornell:

1430.

Maybe there was more to it than who I wanted to be or where I wanted to go. More than simply wanting a degree from my dream school. I mean, after being repeatedly stamped AVERAGE by The Powers That Be, I guess I found myself desperate for some kind of validation.

Validation without a face or a voice.

Only a number.

A perfect score.

(2) Matty

STUDENT I.D. #12215020
GPA 2.3
CLASS RANK 179/281
First S.A.T. score: 920

When I thought about the future, I thought about Sandy. When she left for the University of Maryland, it was one of the hardest times of my life. I always knew she was a year older than me, but I guess I was kind of in denial that she'd have to go.

So I tried to make it like there was as little distance as possible. I took Polaroids of myself and sent them to her. I made her mixes and wrote her at least five e-mails a day.

I told her—I always told her—that I'd be joining her soon.

That was my future.

I wouldn't be like my parents, arguing about their whole lives, calling each other all kinds of messed-up things. I wouldn't be like my father cleaning up other people's shit, riding around in a dirty truck that read MATTHEWS & SON SEPTIC.

He was the MATTHEWS.

I would not be the SON.

I would do okay enough on the S.A.T. I would get into Maryland. Sandy would be waiting for me there. It was all set.

That was my future.

③

Francesca

STUDENT I.D. #12212074
GPA 3.7
CLASS RANK 34/281
First S.A.T. score: BOYCOTTED

I watched things. All the stupid messed-up things people did to one another. All the wrongness. I caught it. I wrote it down. I put it up where anyone could see. Just click on my site and see what's wrong with our stupid, tiny world.

I was tired of it. Tired of pretending. Tired of putting up with people. Tired of dealing with my father and the Pretty Young Things he brought home. That morning, her name was Brittany. He tried to sneak her by me, but it didn't work.

"You know, just because they keep getting younger doesn't mean you will," I told him as he tried to creep back to his bedroom.

He looked at the laptop on my lap. "And

whose life are we ruining today?" he asked. Very funny. Very casual. Very lame.

"Yours," I said. "Or mine. Both probably."

He dismissed me with a chuckle and went to put his shoes on.

To hell with that.

That would not be my future.

(4) Roy

STUDENT I.D. #Not Available
GPA Not Available
CLASS RANK 281/281
First S.A.T. score: Not yet

Dude, it's like . . . whatever.
    You wake. You bake. You make it through.
    That's it.

Desmond

STUDENT I.D. #12215980
GPA Whatever It Takes to Remain Eligible
CLASS RANK First Team All-State
First S.A.T. score: None

You gotta work hard to be the best. Any coach will tell you that. There's talent, sure. There's skill. But there's also work.

Keep your eye on the ball. Keep your feet on the ground. Except for the moments when you're gonna fly.

Mom worked the night shift, so I was the one who got up and made sure Keyon got ready for school. I made the coffee for when Mom got in the door, then I got out the cereals for Keyon. I gave him the choice between Cap'n Crunch and a Wheaties box with Michael Jordan on the front.

"M. J. or the Cap'n?" I asked him,

"M. J.," he answered.

"Good man," I said. He's twelve and he knows right.

I was glad I didn't have practice in the morning. I was glad that I could do this with Keyon, be there when Mom came in.

The rest of the day would be basketball.

And if I played it right, the rest of my life would be basketball.

(6)
Anna

STUDENT I.D. #12215492
GPA 4.0
CLASS RANK 2/281
First S.A.T. score: 1080 CANCELLED

There were only so many hours in the day, and I had to fill them the right way if I wanted to get the things that we all wanted.

I looked at my mother, up early and drinking tea as she worked out on the StairMaster. And my dad, watching CNN and reading the paper at the same time.

"Okay," I told them, as I did every morning, "I'm going."

"What do you have tonight?" Mom asked.

"Helping Hand, a yearbook shoot, and something for Student Council," I told her. "I should be home about six."

You see—every minute accounted for.

"Okay, honey," Daddy said, giving me a peck on the cheek. "Be careful."

And Mom added, "Anna, we're so proud of you."

I nodded. I grinned.

"I know," I said.

And I knew. Every minute, I knew.

I headed to school and saw the same people I had seen for years, but didn't really know. Francesca leaned over her computer and typed something for her Web site. Dez wore his varsity jacket like a billboard of all his accomplishments. A posse of hangers-on followed him wherever he went. I was not a hanger-on. I was a yearbook photographer. And Dez was senior class news. When he met a coach who came all the way from New York, I captured the moment and wondered if this coach was the one who would give Dez his future. I'd been present for so many of his victories. Framing them in the lens.

I was happy when I was taking photographs. But that wouldn't get me into Brown. I needed one more very important element, so I headed for the guidance counselor's office and nervously approached the reception counter. Yes, she was just the receptionist. But I imagined she knew. I imagined everyone knew. I was the fake. I was the mistake. I was the "smart girl" who couldn't do well on the S.A.T., who bailed before she could even finish the test.

"Hi," I said, trying to be casual, trying not to give more of myself away than had already been taken. "Did you get that date yet?"

"The last S.A.T. exam for fall college acceptance is in two weeks," the receptionist droned. "Otherwise you're looking at winter semester."

Not possible.

"No," I said. "I have to have the results for fall."

"Two weeks from Saturday. Sign up here."

She handed me a clipboard.

I signed my life away. One more time.

⑦
Kyle

The term "guidance counselor" was a sick joke, at least in my school. Maybe it worked if you were one of those college-stressed girls who cried her way out of class and got consolation and hall passes from the maternally inclined. They might've gotten guidance. They might've been counseled. But me? I went in there and came out even more lost than before. I'd gotten better "counsel" from fortune cookies.

My guidance counselor was Mr. Dooling. He was easily in his fifties, but claimed he was thirty-nine. He had ten favorite students, and then there were a hundred or so of the rest of us.

"It's a 1020, Mr. Dooling," I said, eyeing the letter with my latest S.A.T. score.

He waited for the punch line. There wasn't one. This wasn't a joke.

This was my life.

"Well, I've seen worse," he said.

"I need a 1430. I've applied to Cornell," I continued.

"What are your fallback schools?" he asked.

My life, I thought. "I don't have any."

And he said, "Kinda risky, isn't it?"

More sifting of my file.

"I mean, I'm looking at your file here, and while your GPA is solid, your P.S.A.T. score wasn't so great, not to mention your Stanfords. Doesn't 1430 seem a bit . . ."

He didn't need to finish the sentence. I could fill it in for him.

Iffy. Unrealistic. Stupid.

Impossible.

I had to explain. Even though he was an idiot—even though this whole thing was idiocy—I had to make him understand.

"Mr. Dooling," I said, "when I was seven years old I made a log cabin out of Popsicle sticks. I'd break the Popsicles off the sticks in the freezer, just so I could work on it. Now you could walk in the halls and five of the first six kids you see won't have a clue about what they want to do with their lives. But I've known since I was seven. I want to be an architect. And when I was old enough to understand that there was one school that turns out the greatest architects of our time, I've wanted to go there. Cornell. It's all I've ever wanted."

For a moment, I thought he got it. That what I said was registering. That he would help me. But no. This system wasn't about help. It wasn't about encouragement.

It was about the scores.

"You know the guy who designed our bus garage attended a community college just down the street," Mr. Dooling told me.

And I wondered if I should just give up.

I knew that if anybody would understand, it would be Matty. Not that he was going through the same thing, but because we'd been best friends for so long. He knew me well. Or at least well enough.

I met him at his locker, which was decorated with photo after photo of Sandy.

I think he saw it all on my face in the first minute. But I gave him the basic rundown, anyway.

"Dooling said you couldn't do it?" he asked. And I loved him for his disbelief, for the fact that he'd been hoping as much as I had.

"Dooling said that standardized testing says I can't do it," I explained.

18

"And you're down to a 1020? Jesus, that's almost as bad as me. What'd you tell your folks?"

"What do you think?"

Telling the truth wasn't something I thought about. It wasn't even a choice. It was that gold star. I imagined my mother putting it there, smiling. I thought of all the sacrifices they had made for me—the way my mom had saved coins in a coffee tin to get me a drawing table, the days my father took off from work to go look at buildings with me.

I couldn't be their failure. Not while there was still even the thinnest of chances.

So I told them I got a 1430. "Son," my dad said, "we've never been so proud."

And that hurt, because there were so many other reasons for them to be proud of me.

And it hurt because it was a total lie.

My mom made me a cake. There were numbered candles on top—1430. I felt like I was made of kerosene. I felt if I got close enough to the candles I would explode.

I knew Matty wouldn't call me on the lie.

"My mom's a teacher, Matty," I added lamely.

"Well," Matty said, "look at the positives." He pressed a finger-kiss to one of the photos and closed the locker. "At least one of us is going to college."

He pulled an envelope out from his back-pack, and his face beamed.

"Hellooooooo, Maryland," he cooed.

I tried to be happy for him. I tried to be happy that he was moments away from joining Sandy in the fall. I tried not to think of myself. It was hard.

We headed back to Matty's house, the sealed envelope a big teaser to the future. We went to our place—the roof. We'd moved an old recliner, a table, and some speakers up there. It was like a fort with no walls. Our escape.

"Maybe I should wait to open it," Matty said once we'd settled in. "I mean, it seems kinda crummy considering your life is falling apart and all."

"Open the letter," I ordered.

"Yeah, you're right. Why should the fact that you're screwed ruin my big day?"

With glee, he tore open the envelope. Unfolded his future. And . . .

His face just crashed.

Along with his life.

⑧
Matty

Oh, shit.

This is not happening.

It couldn't be.

Kyle was good to me. Prevented me from jumping. That kind of thing.

He took me to work so I could get some pay. So I wouldn't get lost in the fact that my chances of getting into Maryland had gone south.

"'S.A.T. score insufficient,'" I kept repeating what the letter had said. "This shit ain't fair. Sandy's gonna be crushed."

"You even know what S.A.T. stands for?" Kyle asked me.

"Suck Ass Test," I told him. This was a game I could get into.

"Scholastic Aptitude Test," he answered, hoisting another box into the trailer. "At least, that's what it originally stood for. Then they changed it to Scholastic Achievement Test. Then they did away with that. You know what it stands for now?"

"What?"

"S.A.T."

"What?"

"S.A.T. stands for S.A.T.," Kyle said. "That's it."

"That's messed up."

Kyle nodded. "Yep."

I was being kept from Sandy by something that meant ABSOLUTELY NOTHING. I started kicking boxes.

"Sever All Ties," I said. "S.A.T. I may as well sever all ties with Sandy."

It didn't seem fair. Not at all.

"There's gotta be someone we can talk to," I said.

9
Kyle

We headed to the Educational Testing Service headquarters, ready to plead our cases. The people behind the test had to be human beings, right? They had to have some compassion, certainly?

Not quite.

The lobby guard blinked back at us from behind a bank of video monitors. It was clear we were keeping him from his very important magazine reading.

"Look," he said gruffly, "do you know how many kids wanna go up to ETS to complain about their S.A.T. scores? If one goes up, they all go up!"

He returned to his magazine. Then this girl from our school—I recognized her, but didn't know her name—showed up and whisked right by.

"But, she—," I protested.

"Unless your father owns the building," the guard said.

It was hopeless.

That night we were back on Matty's roof. He hoisted up a case of Red Bull energy drink that had been delivered by Clyde's Mini-Market.

"Maybe I can get a job at Clyde's," he remarked.

I couldn't take it.

"That's great," I said, slumping in the recliner. "When you pictured your life, were you (a) living at home, (b) riding the bus, (c) making minimum wage, or (d) all of the above?"

Matty shrugged. Giving up.

"S.A.T.," I said, imagining my life as a waiter. "*Share All Tips*."

"So we'll take the test again," Matty said weakly.

"Matt, the retest is in two weeks," I replied. "There's no time to prepare, and even if there was, what's gonna change?"

Matty finished off another can of Red Bull. I wondered what use an good energy drink was if you didn't have anything real to do with the energy.

"I'd better call Sandy," Matty said. I guess that's where all of his energy was going.

He punched in the number, listened for a second, then looked really alarmed. I mean, genuinely freaked out. He hung up without saying a word.

"Some guy answered," he said in this ghostly voice.

"Roommate's boyfriend," I said, trying to calm him down.

"He said, 'Sandy's room.'"

"So?"

"So her roommate is Pam. He'd say, 'Pam's room,' not, 'Sandy's room.' Pam's room. PAM!"

He was in full freak-out mode now. I approached him cautiously, like you would a rabid dog.

"Matt," I said, hoping to draw him back from being crazed. "You're all cranked up. It's the Red Bull, man."

Matty ignored me, pacing the roof like a madman.

"No," he said, "the S.A.T. did this. The S.A.T.'s pimping out my girlfriend."

Then he hurled his phone off the roof, as if it were responsible. "DAMMIT!" he yelled as the phone landed in some bushes. Then he turned to me and continued, "We gotta do something, man. These people are messing with the rest of our lives."

I wasn't really up to being The Voice of Reason, but I figured someone had to do it.

"Matty," I said, "the College Board made twenty-five million dollars last year. You think they give a shit about us?"

"Just hear me out," Matty said. I could tell he was calmer now. This was the usual crazy Matty. "I'm not a dumb guy. I know things. Ask me who's got the best pitching staff in baseball. Or how to rebuild the carburetor on a seventy-one Buick. Ask me what 'icing' is, for christsakes."

"Make the point, Matty."

"The point is, where's that on the test? Because you learn the rest in college. I show up for an internship with some science geek and a couple of math nerds, who gets the job? The guy who can throw down at the water cooler. The guy who's heard the new Ataris record. They guy who yakked in the backseat of your Cutlass after the Radiohead show. I get the job. Not science geek or math boy."

I could only stare at him after that dissertation. "I'm seeing no point."

"The point is," he told me, "they're not playing fair. Why should we? We know where the answers are. ETS. Maybe we should borrow them."

Was he really saying what I thought he was saying?

"You want to steal the answers to the S.A.T.," I said, just making sure.

Matty was on a roll now. Nothing would stop him. To him, it all made perfect sense. "You have a talent, Kyle," he said. "What you can do with a pencil and paper, I could never learn to do. But they have a test you're never gonna pass."

Time for The Voice of Reason again. "A lot of kids struggle with the S.A.T., Matt. It doesn't justify thievery."

Matty was having none of it.

"No?" he chided. "You pass my dad's truck in the driveway when you came up? The one with the large crapper on top. It doesn't say, 'Matthews Septic' on it, Kyle. It says, 'Matthews and Son Septic.' If I don't get into Maryland, my life is shit. Literally. And it's not even my own shit."

He walked to the edge of the roof and pointed down to his neighbor, whose TV blared the latest game show.

"You know why this guy's TV is so loud?" Matty continued. "He's trying to drown out my parents when they start in. Him and me."

I walked over to where he was. Looked into the window. Saw this man hunched over a microwavable dinner.

And what did we see when we looked at him?

We saw what we didn't want to see. What we didn't want.

We saw a possible future.

⑩
Matty

Sitting Alone Tonight.
    Single And Thirty.
    Stubbled And Trembling.
    Sorry Awful Tenant.
    Stuck Around Television.
    Stunned And Trapped.
    Staying A Townie.

·

11

Kyle

Matty was illuminated by the television glow. He looked fired up. Then wired.

Then defeated.

I wanted to console him. I wanted to make everything okay. I wanted everything that was out of reach.

"Matt—," I started to say.

"Shh," he said. "Listen."

From the distant bushes we could hear his phone ringing.

"That might be Sandy," he said. And then he was off, not ready to abandon her call. Not ready to abandon that dream.

Suddenly, it was like glimpsing the future. Seeing the way we would end up. Still loading boxes into trailers. Going through the motions.

Forgetting all the things we'd hoped for. Becoming my brother Larry. Becoming the guy next door. Becoming anyone but who we wanted to be.

And maybe this guy, Matty's neighbor, was happy. Maybe he felt as though his life was full. But looking at him, I couldn't argue with my best friend. Because I saw Matty too. In someone he didn't want to be. And me in Larry, someone I didn't want to be.

I got home and found my brother Larry in our laundry room, playing with the dryer alarm—making it blare so he could "duet" with it on his guitar. It didn't matter that I wanted to study. I wanted to know my future was secure, and he just wanted to find the first chord for "Smoke on the Water," by Deep Purple.

He saw the annoyed look on my face. He'd seen it enough times to know what it meant. "Ya know I worry about you, Kyle," Larry said. "One of these days you're gonna try to recapture a youth you never had."

I turned back to take a good look at him. "Is that what you're doing?" I asked. "Recapturing your youth, living at home, and jamming with the dryer?"

"I live above the garage," Larry said defensively. "It's a separate dwelling." I took a shower and found some of my hair in the drain. I felt older. I felt myself getting older.

My mom was in the living room, correcting homework. How many times had I seen her there, looking at wobbly alphabets and "tests" that asked if the green light meant "go."

"You want to help me grade assignments?" she asked.

I looked down, expecting to see crayon drawings or Magic Marker portraits. But instead I found standardized test answer sheets, with the ovals roughly filled in.

"We're teaching the kids to bubble in," my mother explained.

"First graders," I said. I couldn't believe it.

Mom nodded. Couldn't she see what was wrong with this.

"Mom," I went on, "most of these kids can't even read yet."

Mom sighed. "Well, I hate to say it, but there's more money for the school in bubbling in than reading these days."

That night I dreamed I was taking the S.A.T. in my first-grade classroom. A seven-year-old kid was sitting next to me, bubbling in his answers. The bubbles spelled out HELP ME.

● ○ ○ ○

I couldn't get my mom's words out of my head. I couldn't stop thinking about it.

There it was. Just follow the money. If standardized test scores improved, the schools got more funding.

In some cases, the teachers themselves got bonuses. Like Mr. G, driving his shiny new car with a license plate that read SATS R UP.

Nobody cares what the kids are really learning. Nobody cares about turning them into decent human beings.

No, it was all about the scores.

That was enough to drive me crazy. But it was more than that. I was overcome by the feeling that everything was slipping away. That we were going to be left behind.

The next night at work with Matty, the boxes kept coming, fast and furious. I felt bombarded. Like each box was landing right on top of me. Weighing me down. Crushing me. And each box was filled with expectations. With failures. With systems conspiring against us.

The Panic button was right in front of me. The only way to stop the bombardment.

The only way to struggle against the weight.

I pressed it.

Desperate times called for desperate measures.

We were back on Matty's roof, watching his neighbor watch the same game show as before.

"How would you do it?" I asked Matty.

He looked at me once, making sure I was for real. Then he returned to his watching.

"The girl at ETS," he said. "The one the guard let pass. You recognize her?"

I hadn't known who she was.

But Matty did.

"Francesca Curtis," he said.

The key to our plan.

(12)
Francesca

A lot of kids knew who I was. Not a single one of them knew me. Not a single one.

I had this Web page. My way to expose the wrongness that was Davenport High School. Davenport LIE School, I called it.

It wasn't hard to find wrongness to write about. Like Mr. G-is-for-Greed's stupid new car. TEACHER'S BONUS or TEACHER'S BONE US was my headline. Not subtle. But wrongness isn't subtle, so why should I be?

I got information from people because they were afraid of what would happen if they didn't give it to me. People didn't just come over to chat. I knew that. I was happy about that.

So when the two guys came over to me in study hall, I knew it wasn't a social call.

They wanted something. That was fine.

I wanted more.

"Hey," one of them said.

I didn't even look up. Looking up was not worth my time. "You guys know the name of that sophomore kid with the Percocet addiction?" I asked.

Just the sound of their shrugs in response.

Time to say good-bye.

"Never mind," I said, looking up. "You got something for the page, you need to write it down and slip it in my locker."

"We don't—," one of them sputtered.

"If you can't find my locker, you're in over your head," I interrupted.

There was a beat. Then the other one tried.

"Actually," he said, "we had something else in mind."

Then he told me who they were and started talking about a crazy plan. I heard enough to get the idea. And I wasn't ready to say whether it was a good idea or a bad idea. I just told them it was time to shut up—there were too many people who could listen in study hall. People who weren't distracted.

I made arrangements for a better place to talk. A place where everyone would be distracted.

O O O

That night, we met in the gym, at our school's big basketball game. The players themselves weren't that bad—Desmond Rhodes dominated the floor like he dominated everything else at Davenport. But the crowd was a total joke. Like a political rally for losers.

I was interested in what Kyle and Matty had to say, but not that interested. I used a Sharpie to color Matty's fingernails JUST to see if he'd let me. That was vaguely interesting.

"So you guys are gonna steal the S.A.T. answers?" I asked. From the guys' reaction, you'd have thought I'd just shouted out how big their dicks were. Like anyone was listening.

"You should," I continued. I'd given this a little thought—no more than it merited. "It's anti-girl. I mean, it's anti a lot of shit, but it's definitely got chick issues. You know it underscores girls on verbal and math?"

As soon as I finished talking, Desmond made a power dunk. Kyle leaped to his feet and shouted, "DESMOND RHODES— SUPERSTAR!" with the crowd. He was dressed in a green shirt—our school's sucky color—along with the rest of the pep club. If you looked from far away, all the green shirts spelled out a D for Desmond. It was so bizarre.

I was not going to let that disrupt my thought.

"On top of that," I went on, "the College Board settled a complaint that the P.S.A.T. had testicle bias for National Merit Scholarships. I had that on the page sophomore year."

"So you'll help us, then?" Matty gulped.

Ha!

"Not a chance," I told them.

"Why not?" Matty asked.

Wasn't it obvious?

"Well gosh, Pacey," I snarked, "maybe I don't think you and Dawson can pull it off. Do you have a plan?"

"We're working on it," Kyle said.

Yeah. Right.

"Waste of my time, boys," I told them. It was time for me to go, before the pep spread.

Kyle wasn't giving up. "But don't you find it ridiculous that they tell us from day one to be unique, to be individuals, and then they give us a standardized test and make us all one faceless herd?"

This from a guy in school colors.

"Wait!" he called before I could beat a retreat. He kept talking as he followed me toward the exit. "A hundred million dollars a year on prep materials, probably sixty million of that from girls alone. For what? To pick up a few stones to throw at a bully that doesn't fight fair? Look around this place. How many of these girls are gonna get screwed by this test? What's it going to do to their self-image? On top of everything else they have to deal with."

It was sort of amusing how he was loading it on.

Nice try, Green Boy.

"Think maybe you're kinda preaching to the converted?" I asked.

"I know I am," he admitted. "I mean, that's why we approached you. We need your help."

I looked around at the stupid pepsters, the droning hoards. I thought about breaking and entering. I thought about getting away with it.

"What the hell," I said. "Sounds fun."

(13)

Desmond

You shoot, you score.

You shoot, you score.

And the thought was: You keep shooting, you keep scoring. As long as you choose the right shots.

On the court, off the court—it didn't matter. I always had their attention. I always chose my shots.

The biggest call was about the future: to go to college or to try out straight for the pros.

The coaches kept coming. Flying in from across the country. Talking about my dreams when I knew they were really talking about theirs. Their dream of having me play for them. Being a part of their team.

Most of them met me at the school. We

talked a little, got a picture, shook hands.

The ones who counted came to my house. Talked to my mom. Showed me what they had.

A coach from St. John's came to my game, saw me make all the right moves. Then afterward we went to my house and he showed me a sports magazine. Me on the front, wearing his team's uniform.

"This could be you," Coach Jarvis said. "Whaddya think?"

The headline on the cover read, DEZTINY.

I looked at Keyon, who was all excited. I couldn't help but grin. I really liked the sight of it.

"I look good in red," I said to the man. "But I was thinking more like 76er red."

The coach's smile faded a little.

"Is that why you haven't taken your S.A.T. yet?" he asked. "The pros?"

I shot a look at my Mom. We disagreed on my career path. "We're still weighing our odds," I said. Meaning: I was still trying to figure out my shot.

"May I speak honestly?" Jarvis asked.

"I wish you would," Mom chimed in. She didn't like the no-college idea.

Coach put down the piece of pie Mom had given him and leaned forward. "I want you to

41

come to St. John's, Dez," he said. "Okay? But if you decide we're not for you, I want you to go to college somewhere, because the fact of the matter is, your game's not ready."

I was not hearing that. Clearly, the man had not been paying attention.

He went on. "Son, you have an amazing amount of talent on the basketball floor. But it's not NBA talent. Yet. Now you're three years away from the NBA Developmental League age requirement, so ask yourself this: Do I play overseas or on national television? Do I go to some IBL outpost, or do I go to the Final Four?"

I picked up a basketball and spun it in my hand.

"You have a dream," Coach Jarvis told me. "I respect and admire that. And I promise you this: If you come to St. John's, we'll do everything we can to get you to the NBA. But more than that, you'll have a college degree in hand should any of us fall short."

"That's what I'm talking about," Mom said in that tone she gets.

I shot her a look. We'd talked about this before. Over and over again.

"Where do we go from here?" I said to the guy from St. John's, trying to get us back on track.

"Well, that's up to you," he said. "Your

GPA's on the low end for us, but we can work with that. We just need you to get us a nine hundred or better on the S.A.T."

I wasn't all that into having Keyon around for the rest of this conversation, so I asked him to be the man and grab me a drink. Once he was gone, I asked Coach what I had to ask.

"The S.A.T.," I said. "Is there any way around that?" If anyone would know, I was sure a big-time coach would.

"Desmond," my mom said, voice full of warning.

"I'm just asking," I said. "I hear things."

Coach Jarvis smiled at me. All fatherly.

"If I told you there was," he said, "would I really be the kind of coach you'd want to play for? A nine hundred, Desmond. That's it."

Like it's that simple.

Like it's a shot I can score.

14

Anna

There was an ambush when I got home from the basketball game. His name was Tom.

All I wanted to do was put my camera away and get some sleep. It had been a long day in a string of long days. But Mom was waiting for me, with Daddy and a man I'd never seen before sitting behind her.

"Here she is," Mom said. "Did the game run late, honey?" She turned to this strange man and explained the camera. "She's the yearbook photographer."

Like I was out with friends partying on a Friday night. Like that was even an option.

"Um, yes," I said. "A little."

"Anna," Daddy said, moving closer, "this is

Tom Hackett. Tom's an old friend who might be able to help us with Brown."

Tom stood up and extended a hand.

"It's a pleasure to meet you, Anna," he said. I was sure he'd heard a million great things about me. Things I couldn't begin to live up to.

"Hi," I said. Mom took my camera out of my hands, and Daddy sat me down, next to Tom.

"So Anna," the man—my parents' age—said. "What types of things interest you besides photography?"

"Tell him about the pledge drive you coordinated," Mom prompted.

I was not in the mood for this. But it was Brown, so I ventured an answer.

"We asked students to sign a pledge to refrain from drug use," I began.

"It was very successful," Daddy finished, before I'd really started.

"That's great," Tom said. I wondered if he had any real desire to listen to all of this, or if this was just another favor. A favor for me.

"She's also involved in several other community related projects," Mom went on.

And so it continued. Mom and Daddy talking about my achievements without me getting out a full sentence. Tom using every form of "that's great" he could think of. Me thinking of Brown, of my campus visit there, of how I could picture myself in Providence, playing Frisbee on the Green, grabbing a pizza at this snack bar called the Gate that the tour guide told us about. I pictured myself in the tour guide's life, having her classes, hanging out with her friends.

And then I remembered my S.A.T. scores. If I told them to Tom, he wouldn't say "that's great." He'd just call me a freak, and we'd be done.

I made it through, as I always make it through. Trying to create the perfect photograph of myself.

Later, once Tom was gone, I retreated to my bedroom. I scrutinized my well-worn S.A.T. prep manual. I looked over the sheet listing all the clubs and activities I had mapped out for the month.

I had so much to do.

And nothing to do.

Mom knocked on my door and came in. "I thought that went well," she said. She was about to say something else but was distracted by the sound of a car streaming past—all these kids hollering and happy because of the final score of the game. Mom crossed to the window and closed it.

"I guess we won," she said.

"Yeah," I said. "They did."

Mom leaned over and brushed my hair from my face. "You know," she said, voice all comforting, "your father and I have noticed the effort you've put into this retest."

"What if I mess up again?" I couldn't help but ask.

"You won't," Mom said. "You're going to do great. We're proud of you, honey."

If only getting the results could have been as easy as getting her reassurance. After she left the room, I pulled out a Brown Directory I'd swiped during my campus visit. Every now and then I had to do this.

I looked at the list of names. Some I'd crossed out. Others I'd highlighted, with notes. It was always the same kind of conversation.

I dialed the next number. My heart raced a moment before someone picked up. "Hi," I said. "Who is this?"

"Cleo," a girl answered. "Who is this?"

Cleo. I liked that name.

"Cleo?" I said. "I think I dialed the wrong number, but you sound familiar. What's your Thursday morning class?"

"M.E. lecture," Cleo said.

"M.E. lecture?" I echoed. I had no idea what that was. "Mine too. Well, I'm sorry to bother you, but—oh hey, before I let you go, my roommates and I are having this discussion right now. Maybe you can help."

"Sure," Cleo said. Brown students can be so helpful.

Now it was time for the big question. "What's the lowest S.A.T. score you ever heard of anyone who got into Brown?"

15
Matty

I was thinking, *Right, we can do this.* I mean, Francesca's dad owned the building. Kyle was, like, this brilliant designer. And I—well, I wanted it bad. What could go wrong?

Then the next day—the day after Francesca had decided she wasn't too good for us—Kyle caught me by the sinks in the boy's room and started the conversation with, "Hey, Matty, don't freak out, okay?"

Now, I wasn't a fool. I knew when someone started off like that, odds were they had something freak-out worthy to say.

"About what?" I asked, trying not to let my blood pressure rise.

"Just don't," Kyle said, knowing me too well.

"I won't," I said. "What's up?"

Kyle checked under the stalls for people who might be there. Then, when he was sure we were alone, he said, "Did you see the photographer at the game? The girl on the baseline?"

Sure, I'd seen her. Anna Ross. Big old dork. Always holding her camera.

"Yeah," I said, not having any idea where he was going with this. "I saw her. Why?"

"Well, I told her."

I couldn't believe it.

"YOU TOLD ANNA ROSS?!" I shouted. Then I began to pace.

"You said you wouldn't freak out," Kyle reminded me.

"That was before I knew you told the class brain," I told him.

"Well, I'm sorry. But did you ever think we're not the only ones in this boat?"

"What boat?" I yelled back. "It's ANNA ROSS!"

I was pissed. No doubt about it.

But I could also tell there was something else. There had to be some reason why.

"What'd she say, anyway?" I asked.

(16)
Kyle

Sure I'd seen her before. But I hadn't really noticed her. Anna Ross. She always had her camera in front of her eyes, so I'd never noticed they had a color. I'd never noticed how pretty she was, or that there was something in her expression that you just trusted.

I waited for her. After the game. If you'd asked me then, I wouldn't have been able to tell you why I was still there. But in the chaos after the victory, as everyone was cheering and she was taking her last shots, I found myself trailing her. Then standing next to her. Then talking.

We talked about the game. Then I asked her about her photos. I asked her where she was going to school in the fall. I mean, Anna Ross.

Top of the class. Star student. There was no way she wasn't already into college.

Except, yes. There was a way. And I saw it in her eyes—that fear. I remembered her now from the first time I'd taken the S.A.T. I remembered her leaving before the test was over. Knowing she was doing badly, and abandoning it.

The whole story came out. As the crowd dispersed, as kids and adults cheered for Dez and recounted all his plays, I told her a little bit of our plan. It's not like I made a conscious decision to include her, no more than I'd made a conscious decision to talk to her. It just happened.

"You know, I don't even know you," she said. "And even if I did, what you're talking about is wrong. It's cheating."

"It's a victimless crime," I argued.

Think about it. Who would get hurt? If a few of us scored higher than usual, it wouldn't affect the curve. It wouldn't shift the "percentiles." Nobody else would score lower because we had an edge.

I could feel Anna's gaze on me. Scrutinizing. Trying to figure me out.

"Hypothetical situation," she said. "You're driving, it's late, and you come to a red light in the middle of nowhere. Not a soul around. It's a victimless crime. Do you run the light and break the rules?"

I thought about it. Before I could answer, she continued, "You see, you don't. You wait. Because a victimless crime is still a crime. It's not worth it."

No doubt about it—she was smart. But there was still room to maneuver.

"Maybe it is," I countered. "Maybe I run it. It depends."

"On what?" she asked.

"Am I trying to get somewhere important?" She nodded.

Got her, I thought.

Now, I knew Matty would freak out about my telling her, but I also hoped he'd figure I wouldn't have done it if it hadn't seemed like the right thing to do.

As I told him the story, I could see his anger leveling off. I mean, he was still pissed off. But it wasn't going to get worse than that.

"So she's in," he said when I was done.

"She said no," I told him. I hadn't really gotten her, after all.

"But she knows about it," Matty pointed out. I shrugged, which only made him go on the offense more. "You like this girl?" he asked.

"Matt," I warned. This was not the issue.

"No," he said, warming up to the idea. "Because I could see if you were trying to get into her pants."

"It wasn't like that," I told him. Because it wasn't. It really wasn't. "I just get the feeling . . . something tells me she needs this as bad as we do."

"Something tells you?" Matty's annoyance was turning to mockery now. "To walk up to Anna Ross and invite her to break into ETS and steal the S.A.T. answers. Some inner voice signed off on this."

"Yeah," I said, getting annoyed. "All right? And for your information, we're not all hen-pecked."

I had Matty on the defense now.

"Whaddaya saying?" he challenged.

Did I have to spell it out?

"You, Sandy, Maryland." I paused. "Maybe you don't really want to go to Maryland?"

That got him. He sneered at me, then kicked a stall door angrily. The door crashed back . . . into someone. There was a thud and a groan.

Someone had heard us.

Nervously I pushed open the door and came face-to-face with Roy. Stoned out of his mind but still registering everything we said.

(17)
Roy

Breaking into the freakin' ETS.

Brilliant. Freakin' brilliant.

I was so into it. No way I couldn't be a part of it.

Shit like this doesn't come along every day, you know.

(18)
Francesca

So I ended up as Nancy Drew to this bunch of Hardly Boys.

Pathetic.

The next night we headed over to my father's building. It was nice to know that my dear old daddy was good for something other than picking up Petty—I mean, Pretty—Young Things. I'd been coming to this building since I was little, coming in for Take Our Daughters to Work Day on the few occasions it wasn't also Take My Secretary to Acapulco Week. Since my father never had anything for me to actually do when I was around, I'd wandered through the halls a lot. That would help us.

So there we were, Nervous Kyle, Lughead

Matty, and Spaceboy Roy, looking over the corporate tower.

"ETS has the entire top floor," I explained.

Kyle looked like he was about to take notes. "Can you get us up there?" he asked.

That, I figured, would be the least of his problems.

"Probably," I said. "But then what?"

Kyle nodded, acknowledging, I guess, that we needed some kind of plan beyond knowing what floor the tests were on.

"I don't know yet," he admitted. "But we're not talking about a big heist. It's as simple as getting in, finding the answers, making a copy, and getting out. We just gotta figure out the easiest way to do it."

Okay. That was a start.

We scanned the buildings from our cover in the trees. A large crow hovered on a branch above our heads. So freaking Poe.

"CAW!" Roy screeched, and it flew off. The most coherent thing Roy had said all night.

The crow clearly had taste in men. It flew off.

Roy looked pleased. Like he'd just pissed in a pool or something.

"You've assembled a crack team, chief," Matty said sarcastically.

Cracked, maybe.

"Well, what was I supposed to do?" Kyle said, well on his way to exasperation. "He threatened to bust us. And he knows everything."

"So does Anna Ross," Matty said. "But she's not here."

It was like the blind leading the blind. First Bongwater Brain, and then Priss-illa, Queen of the Deserted?

"You told Anna Ross?" I asked. I just needed to confirm this act of stupidity.

"He had a 'feeling' about her," Matty reported.

"Was the feeling anywhere near your crotch?" I said.

It was a rhetorical question. I knew the answer, and it reflected as badly on Kyle as it did on the whole situation.

But I wasn't going to dwell on it. We were here to do something, and I'd started to want it bad. To mess with the S.A.T. was to mess with The System on a grand scale.

We just needed a way in.

Then it hit me.

"Guys," I said. "I have an idea."

Tomorrow they were going to take a little tour. In disguise.

o o o

Now, there was no way I was going to pass my stooges off as executives, or even executive assistants. There was only one group of workers in the whole building who were close to our age. The mail guys. I knew this because I'd been checking them out for as long as I knew that guys and girls were different. I still had dreams about Michael, a guy who worked on the sixth floor last year. Every now and then we'd make out in the supply closet off the mailroom, where the uniforms were kept. So I got Kyle and Matty dressed and ready to go undercover.

I had no idea where Roy was. I wondered if he had any idea either. We commandeered a mail bin and headed for the freight elevator. I could tell Matty wanted to ride inside the cart.

"The mail room services the entire building," I explained to the boys. "And they hire a lot of guys straight out of high school."

The great thing about executives is that they rarely pay attention to their mail guys. Our advantage.

As the elevator doors opened, I reminded Matty and Kyle, "They won't know you. Just act like you own the place."

"Easy for you to say," Matty mumbled. "You do."

Idiot. "Do you want to know what we're up

59

against or not?" I asked angrily. Then I relented a little and told them they'd be fine.

I wished I could go along with them. Help them out. They certainly needed it. But there was a definite chance I'd be recognized. The elevator doors closed with them inside; the boys were on their own.

19

Matty

Freight elevators move very slowly. There was plenty of time for me and Kyle to realize what we were getting ourselves into.

"Cornell still worth it?" I asked.

"Yeah," Kyle said. "Sandy?"

"Yep."

"Good. 'Cause we're in it now."

I tried to think about what Francesca had said. Just act like you own the place. But what did that mean? The only place I'd ever owned was a fishbowl. And even that I'd managed to drop.

We made it to the top floor. The doors opened, and Kyle took a deep breath. He pushed forward, and I followed.

Sandy, I kept thinking. *Sandy, Sandy, Sandy.*

We wheeled the mail cart into the ETS reception area.

I own the place. I own the place. I own—

"Can I help you?" the receptionist asked, like she owned the place.

I froze.

Yes, you can help us . . . just give us the S.A.T. answers to copy.

No way. No how.

I figured Kyle would know what to say, but he was as speechless as I was.

Then Roy appeared—in total mail gear.

"These are the new mail room slaves," he said, all assurance. Then he turned to us and said, "You guys forgot your badges."

He handed us some IDs and looked like he wasn't too happy with us. Like we were totally brain dead.

It was easy to play along with that.

"Now let's go, losers," he continued. "Pay attention."

So we followed him. The receptionist didn't question us.

We wheeled the cart into a vacant corridor.

"What are you doing here, Roy?" Kyle asked.

"You mean other than bailing you out?" he said.

"How'd you get in?" I added.

"I'm the ghost," Roy replied. As if that explained everything.

Then he surprised me again and tugged off his mail smock.

"By the way," he said, "mail pickup was this morning." Then he tossed his smock into the cart and headed out. Leaving us.

It took a second for me to figure it out. If the mail had already been delivered, our disguise was totally worthless.

Kyle figured this out too. We took off our smocks. We had made it inside—but now we were going to have to make it up as we went along.

We had to find that test. Those answers.

Nothing short of that.

Not for me. Not for Kyle.

Not for Sandy.

Kyle went left. I went right.

It was strange to be in an office. I mean, a place where everyone was working, and there was no heavy-lifting or septic pumping involved. Just offices with doors and people working behind them. Cubicles and computers with screen savers that had random sayings scrolling across them.

I felt like a total outsider. In enemy territory.

I walked carefully. Kept my head down and my eyes open. Then I saw it. The water cooler. I'd always thought the water cooler was the great equalizer—a man could survive on conversation alone. Sure, these people had office jobs and were wearing ties and were responsible for all the standardized hell that students across the country were being put through. But I could still bond with them. I was sure of it.

I walked over to a woman and two guys by the water cooler and said hey.

"Hi," the woman said. A start.

I figured I should launch right in. "So," I said. "You guys heard the new Ataris CD?"

All three of them shook their heads. Confused. Having no idea what I was talking about. I would not give up. Maybe they were just a little behind on the musical times.

"No?" I went on. "Well, how 'bout that game last night?"

Nothing. Just glazed looks.

Then they all walked away. To their offices. To their cubicles.

I was a nobody to them. I hadn't made the grade.

Again.

20

Anna

I tried not to think about what Kyle had said. It was ridiculous. Impossible. Too big a risk. Instead, I pulled out my S.A.T. study guides. I made the same vows I'd made a thousand times before: to push harder, to do better, to avoid— well, to avoid what had happened before. My S.A.T. meltdown.

I still had to do my student tutoring. But even there I tried to cram as many obscure vocab words into my head as humanly possible. I mean, they were the same words I'd memorized last time. But when I took the test, I only remembered the flash cards in flashes. And there were always words I'd never seen before. Always.

My mind was somewhere between "capricious" and "spurious" when I heard a voice above me say, "Waiting till the last minute?"

I'd know that voice anywhere, especially coming from that height.

Desmond.

"Oh," I said. "Hi."

I pulled a folder of photos from my bag and handed it to Dez. He looked over the shots. They weren't bad. I liked taking photos of Dez. There was always something going on with him, even if it wasn't what it first appeared. Sometimes, when he made a slam dunk, you'd see his triumph. But other times, if you looked really closely, you would also see the tension. The work of it.

"Nice," Desmond said, pleased. "Remember that dunk I had like this, freshman year? My first big jam? You took the picture after I landed."

"Plus, it was out of focus," I reminded him.

"Now look at you," he said, dismissing my doubts like he dismisses his own. "Thanks, A."

He started for the door, and I returned to my study guide. Then he turned back and said, "You think you could help me with that?"

"Photography?"

"No. That." He pointed to the S.A.T. manual.

I shrunk back. "No," I said. "I can't."

How could I help someone at something I kept failing? I liked Dez a lot—don't get me wrong. I would've helped him out on anything else. Homework, sure. Study for a bio test, absolutely. But not this. It was like I felt bombing the test was contagious. I was the No. 2 Pencil kiss of death.

But Dez was persistent. He wasn't going to let me off so easy.

"C'mon, Anna," he said, "I know you gotta have mad smarts to be a student tutor."

"But there's not enough time," I argued. "The exam's next week. And, anyway, I thought you were going pro. Didn't you say that?"

"Yeah well," he said, offhand, "my mom has her heart set on college. You know how moms are."

I did. Of course I did. When I was six, my mother made me this small pillow that I could hang on my doorknob. IVY LEAGUE BOUND, it read. Bound like I was going there. Bound like I was tied to it.

And I thought of Desmond's mom. I had taken her picture once, cheering on the sidelines. You could see how proud she was. She was screaming at the top of her lungs. But there was this one moment—he landed a little off, wobbling on his knee. I took the picture then, and you could see the fear on her face. When the joy faded, the concern was there. Bound.

"I'm sure you'll do fine," I told Dez. But

even I could tell it sounded weak.

"Nah," he said. "I won't. I mean, if it was just math, maybe. Math doesn't scare me. It breaks you down the same, no matter what your game is. Two plus two is hard to argue, right? It's the rest of it that scares me."

"It all scares me," I confessed.

"And you're what? White girl, top ten in the class." He looked me over, doubtful for both of us. "C'mon. No way I beat this thing. They know it, and so do I."

"You ever heard the term 'stereotype vulnerability'?" I asked him. One look on his face told me he hadn't. "It means that some students do badly on the S.A.T. only because they know they're expected to."

"Yeah?" Desmond said. "Well, I'll tell you something about stereotype vulnerability: You mess up on the S.A.T., you gotta live with it, your parents maybe. But if I do? I gotta read about it in *USA Today.*"

He held up my photo of his slam dunk and mocked a headline, "Desmond Rhodes is a Dumb-Ass."

It was a hard thing to hear because I could tell he honestly believed it.

We had been friends ever since that first blurry photo. I had always felt I was different from his other fans. With them, he always acted a little above, a little aloof. But with me, he was just Desmond. He could be as close to his true self as he would let himself be. Now what he was showing me was even closer than that. And I didn't know what to do with it.

"You know," he continued, "because I can play ball, teachers have been letting me slide since forever. I'm not saying it's their fault, 'cause it's not. I did what I did. But if I could just find a way to get past this thing . . . it all means more to me now. That's all I'm saying."

There were places he wanted to go. Dreams he had. We had that in common.

And there was one thing standing in his way. Just one thing.

Half of it verbal. Half of it math.

I knew I was thinking things I shouldn't have been thinking. But there was some part of me that was saying to go for it. To try. And the reason I listened to that part was because it wasn't about just me anymore. It was about more than me.

"Desmond," I said. "There's this guy I met. . . ."

(21)

Kyle

So much of life is being at the right place at the right time and faking it.

I walked through ETS without a clue about what to do. I didn't know where to start looking. I didn't even really know what I was looking for.

I passed glass-walled office after glass-walled office. I started to worry about finding my way out. And then this guy—a good Worker Bee—waved me into his office.

Arnie Branch, his door said. Office 545.

"Copy room, right?" Arnie asked me.

"Um . . . right," I replied.

Faking it.

The man handed me a bunch of papers, no doubt thinking I was the latest lackey sent his way.

"Great," he said. "I need three copies of this on rush. One comes back to me. One goes to Anne Clark. And the master goes to 510 for filing. Got it?"

"Sure," I said.

Of course I had no idea where the copy room was. Or where anything else was, for that matter. But I didn't let him see me sweat. And believe me, I was sweating. The guy had just handed me the S.A.T. master answer sheet.

I circled around for a little while, looking for the copy room. Finally, I found it, and Matty just outside.

"Check it ou—what are you doin'?" I asked him.

"Casing the place," he answered, snack in hand. He'd managed to find the vending machines, if nothing else. "Right?"

I shook my head and showed Matty what had fallen right into our laps. Or hands, as the case may be.

"God bless America," Matty said, exhaling.

I tried to think rationally. "If we take it," I said, "they might get suspicious. They could change it by next Saturday."

The answer was clear.

"Copy it," we both said.

Hastily, before someone walked in and our luck was ruined, I shoved the exam answers into a large feeder. I grinned and hit the green button to start the copying.

"Say hello to your future, Matty."

Only it wasn't copied. It was shredded.

It wasn't a copier. It was a shredder.

So much of life is being at the right place at the right time and not screwing it up.

(22)
Matty

Shredded And Totaled.

We got out of there.

Someone Alter Time.

We met Francesca outside and just looked up at ETS at the top of that big building.

Septic And Toilets.

I thought of my dad's truck pulling up. I imagined my future sputtering into the driveway.

Suddenly Absolutely Traumatized.

"C'mon, man," Kyle said. "It was a good run."

Suffer Actions Terribly.

"What run?" I spat out. "There was no run."

"Well, whatever it was, it's over now," Francesca said matter-of-factly.

Kyle's expression fell. He gave up.

That night after work, his expression changed a little. He saw someone waiting. Anna.

I wondered what she wanted, and I tried to look on the bright side. "At least she didn't bring the cops."

(23)
Kyle

How can you look forward to something when you don't know it's coming? I never imagined she would find me there. I never imagined she'd show up at all.

She said she wanted to talk, so we walked away from Matty. She didn't have to tell me, because I already knew: She wanted to be a part of it. That much was clear.

It was everything else that was confusing.

"If I wanted to do what we talked about," she began, "would you need to know why?"

She was very pretty when she was vulnerable.

"No," I answered. "But I don't think that's going to be possible."

"Oh," she said with a sigh, spirits falling even further.

"Can I ask you something?" I said. "Why did you bail on the exam?" I asked.

"I didn't," she said defensively, guarded.

I'd seen her there. I knew she'd done it.

"I saw your answer sheet. It was practically blank."

Anna looked away. Steeling herself. Wanting to tell me. Debating it. Then going for it.

"A woman boards a train at midnight," she started.

I listened, waiting for more. She noticed this, then continued.

"I was doing fine until I came to a story question. 'A woman boards a train in New York at midnight. Three hours later, a man also boards.' And for some reason, I couldn't get past it. That probably sounds crazy, but for me it hit home, and I wanted to be on that train. Just be gone for a night to somewhere—I don't know—less practical. Or at least less certain."

Anna hung her head like it was happening all over again. "Anyway, I guess I froze. But when I got home, I realized how disappointed my parents would be." She looked up, right in my eyes. "I have to do great on this test, Kyle."

How many times had I thought the same thing? But we'd lost our chance.

"Yeah, well, like I said," I sputtered.

"If it's money you want, we could pay you."

I started to tell her it wasn't about money. Then I realized the pronoun she'd used.

"We?" I asked.

"There's someone else besides me. Please don't say no."

I couldn't help it. She was so pretty and so vulnerable. And she wanted it so badly that I suddenly wanted it again.

So I said yes.

Matty was another matter. I dragged him to the gym for another basketball game. So he could see the latest member of our team.

"No!" he yelled.

He wasn't taking it all that well.

"C'mon, Matt," I pleaded.

"What in the hell is wrong with you?" he shot back.

"It's just one more person."

"It's Desmond Rhodes! Besides, I heard he was going pro."

"Nah," a voice next to us said. Roy's voice. He wasn't just a ghost—he was a shadow.

"He's not strong enough to be a four and not quick enough to be a three," Roy went on. "Besides, he's got no left hand, and his mid-range game needs work. I don't see it."

Thank you, Mr. SportsCenter.

Matty would not be distracted. "Anna Ross is bad enough," he said. "But do you know how high-profile Desmond Rhodes is?"

I wasn't going to argue about Desmond Rhodes's popularity. We weren't asking him to be an undercover spy. That wasn't the question here. So I told Matty, "Well, he knows about it and he wants in. And Anna says he needs it and we can trust him."

"'Anna says he needs it!' What are we, a freaking soup kitchen?"

Roy chuckled. Matty and I both sneered at him. He was the weakest link here. We didn't really need his scorn as well.

"Which brings me to point number two," Matty said, unstoppable in his disagreement. "Last I heard, we had no way of doing this."

But I'd been thinking about that.

I had another plan.

Francesca

You've got to respect the dog that gets back up after being kicked. So when Kyle called me and said he needed me to steal some plans from my father, I said sure.

The two of us met at my favorite coffee-house. I had everything he needed wrapped up in a poster tube. It was almost too easy—my father never locks his study because he figures all the secrets happen in the bedroom. It would never occur to him that I would take any interest in his business—even to use it against him.

"Was your father suspicious?" Kyle asked.

"To be suspicious you'd have to be interested," I pointed out. Clearly, Kyle wouldn't understand. Clearly he had parents who occasionally acted like parents.

"There are door codes, too," Building Boy added. "They have to supply the building owner with them in case of emergency."

"I can get 'em," I said. No problem.

"All right," Kyle said, getting up. "I'll see you Tuesday."

I figured that would be it. I certainly didn't want any more. But you can't stop a Dawson from being a Dawson.

"Francesca," Kyle added. "That bad, huh?"

I was not about to have this conversation. Everything I was going to give him was in that poster tube.

"My father?" I said. "Whatever. The poor rich girl is kinda played out, don't you think? I mean, that's the oldest story in the world, isn't it?"

"Not if it's your story," he said.

What does that mean? I wondered. By asking the question, I didn't have to realize I knew the answer.

"Hey," I said, ready to turn the conversation back to him. "What do you tell yourself when that little voice says you're being selfish? That it's not about fighting the S.A.T. as much as you wanting what you want?"

"I tell myself I'm helping Matty."

"So Matty's the selfish one."

"Nah. He tells himself he's helping me."

I knew at once that was the truth.

"Tuesday night, then," I said.

I'd be there. I was willing to be part of the truth.

(25)
Kyle

And sometimes it's that easy. Misguided, maybe, but easy.

Things happen. People join the cause. And you find yourself moving toward something you didn't plan on approaching.

Only by the time you're aware of it, the plans of one become plans of six.

And the plans of six become one.

Francesca got me the layout of the building. Blueprints are written in a language I can read fluently. I saw openings and entrances, dead ends and hazards.

Anna staked out the building with her camera. She captured the comings and goings. She mapped out the security in a different way—with a lens.

Desmond stayed out of it. We didn't want the attention he'd bring. Instead he played basketball like he always played basketball. He dreamed of playing for St. John's like it was his best future.

Matty tried to reach Sandy. He wouldn't tell her he was risking it all for her. But he was risking it, anyway.

Roy slept. Played video games. Stayed invisible.

We all did our thing. But this time, we were doing our thing for a greater purpose.

When Francesca sent out the e-mail telling us when to meet, she called us the S.A.T. Study Group.

Roy

Dude, I'd never been in a study group before.

Tuesday came around and I was ready for it. Stoked.

Was racking up a high score on my PlayStation when I realized it was time. Called my man Desmond on his cell phone.

"WASSSSSSSSSUPPPPPPPP!!!?" I greeted, all friendly like.

"Who is this?" the big basketball star asked.

"It's Roy. From the S.A.T. Thing," I explained.

"How'd you get this number?" Big Shot asked.

"I'm the ghost, man," I told him.

The man nobody sees. The man nobody knows. Drifting through a hallway near you.

I heard a shuffle on the other line. And then this woman's voice, asking, "Who's calling, please?"

I eyed my speakerphone. Bad vibes, dude. Bad vibes were coming into my PlayStation. I picked up the receiver.

"It's, um," I said. She almost made me forget my name. Then finally I got it. "Roy."

"Well, Roy," she barreled ahead, "this is our dinnertime. We don't interrupt your dinnertime, do we?"

"I don't have a dinnertime," I said. (It was true.)

"Well, that is a shame. But you can't expect the rest of the world to live like wild dogs. You have some business with my son?"

Now, calling me a wild dog was going too far. But she was scary, and that was just on the phone. I didn't want to see what she was like in person, so I politened myself up.

"Well, ma'am," I said, trying to be smooth and respectful, "I'm at this time assisting him with his S.A.T. exam preparations, and I was hoping he could possibly pick me up this evening as I'm currently without transportation . . . at the present time."

"S.A.T.," she repeated. Clearly I'd used the right phrase. "Well, Roy, there's hope for you yet. Give me the address."

"I appreciate that, ma'am. And may I say

you have an attractive voice. Very pleasant. Young sounding."

"Mmhmm," she said. I was doing well, but I couldn't scam her about everything. I told her my address, and she told me Desmond would be there.

I could only imagine the look on his face when she said that.

It was like in that lame-ass movie *Space Jam*. Michael Jordan hanging out with Marvin the Martian.

Unfortunately Desmond's mom had thrown me from my game. I shut the system down and waited for The Man They Call Dez to arrive. I wondered what you were supposed to wear to an S.A.T.-crashing party. I sniffed my pits and figured what I was wearing was fine.

Mr. Hoops arrived in a mighty nice ride—dude was driving an Escalade that probably cost more than my house.

I could tell he was really happy to see me. Looked like he was afraid he'd lose his scholarships just for being seen with me.

I rocked myself into the ride, belted myself in, and checked it out. Fine leather interiors. Top-of-the-line sound system. Shame to let that go to waste, so I cranked up the hip-hop.

"Sweet!" I yelled over the noise. "What school gave you this?"

Man, I should've played basketball.

Desmond lowered the volume and said, "This is my uncle's ride."

"What school gave it to your uncle?" I asked.

That got me a scowl. Not exactly a magazine-cover look.

"The hell you mean, you're the ghost?" Desmond challenged. I was actually kinda touched he'd been listening to me.

"At school," I told him. "I hear things and see things, but nobody sees or hears me."

"You think so," Desmond said. Skeptical.

"I got your cell number, didn't I?"

"So?"

I smiled. "You got mine?"

Desmond threw the car into drive. We didn't talk for the rest of the way.

I disappeared into the seat.

(27)
Kyle

This was it. Our big meeting. Our last chance.

I'd looked at the blueprints for so long that I pretty much had them memorized. At first I hadn't been able to find a way for us to get the exam. Then slowly it came to me. The odds were still way against us. But with a little luck (and an absence of paper shredders), we just might pull it off.

It would depend on all of us. Every single one.

I had no desire whatsoever for my parents to hear what we were planning, so I'd arranged with Larry for the S.A.T. Study Group to meet up in his apartment over the garage.

Matty came over a little early. Moral support, you know. We both needed to psych each other up.

At eight o'clock we headed out to the garage. I had the blueprints. Matty had his mandatory four-pack of Red Bull.

"Tell me again why we should trust these people," Matty said. I was a little amazed that someone who could be so trusting of Sandy could have so little faith in everyone else.

"Why should they trust us?" I pointed out.

"Us? Why wouldn't they trust us?"

At that moment, the murmur I'd been hearing in the background began to rise. Far-off noise coming closer and closer. Coming from Larry's apartment.

Party noise.

"Oh no," I said, gasping.

I'd been hearing a variation of this noise for most of my life. Larry was eight years older than me—when I was in third grade, he was throwing parties in our backyard when our parents were out and he was supposed to be baby-sitting. Now, I liked a good party as much as the next guy. But Larry's parties were always too much for me, especially lately when they'd be full of other guys living at home, other classmates of Larry's who'd never left town. Like their lives were a record playing the same groove over and over again.

We walked in, and the scene was so familiar. The faces were so familiar.

Sad.

Not surprising. Only, it wasn't supposed to be happening now.

Larry walked past, and I grabbed him.

"Larry," I shouted over the noise. "What the hell is this? You said I could have the place tonight."

He looked at me blankly. "Was that tonight? Sorry, man. It's Wine-Tasting Tuesday."

I looked around the room. It wasn't all the usual suspects. There was Roy, sipping a glass of red.

"'Sup?" he asked, happy as a white cloud.

Matty nudged me and pointed to Larry's futon, where poor Anna was wedged between two of Larry's fiend-friends. Desmond sat uncomfortably across from them.

I was about to wonder where Francesca was—bumming some chewing tobacco from Larry's collection?—when she walked in with a box of binders.

"Wow," she said, highly amused. "What's this?"

"Wine-Tasting Tuesday," Matt announced.

"Nice." Francesca clearly approved. She dumped the binders on Matty and plunged right in.

"Larry," I said. "You promised."

"Yeah," he said. "Okay."

There was no way to clear out the "wine-tasting" crowd. So instead we piled into Larry's bedroom . . . with all the coats. Every now and then a new guest would throw a coat in and hit one of us. I tried to imagine what my revenge on Larry would be like. But first we had to do the S.A.T. thing.

The chaos of the party was right outside the door. I could tell Roy, at the very least, would be migrating back if I didn't keep his interest. So I launched right in.

I unfurled the blueprint and said, "All right. This is ETS."

Another jacket was thrown in—right on the blueprint. I shoved it aside and apologized, explaining that there'd been a misunderstanding.

As I sifted through the other plans, Anna opened a notebook and prepared to take notes. Francesca then decided to do the same with her laptop.

"What the hell's she typing?" Desmond asked. Francesca's laptop made even the most popular kids nervous.

"Just taking notes," she explained.

I took out photos of the building and showed one to our group.

"All right," I said again. "This is ETS—"

"Where'd you get the photo?" Francesca interrupted.

"Anna took it," I explained.

Francesca nodded and typed some more. Now it was Anna's turn to grow alarmed.

"I'm not sure I'm comfortable with this," she said.

"Really?" Francesca shot back. "You look comfortable in your Old Navy cotton pullover. Ya gotta get this look!"

Anna looked more vulnerable than ever. Totally unprepared for venom of any kind. "Did I do something?" she asked.

Francesca was relentless. "Yeah," she snarked. "You did something. You got a 4.0 GPA."

"Stop it, Francesca," Matty jumped in. Like I should have.

"You know what the fatal flaw is for most heists?" Francesca continued. "Trusting the team. So pardon me for being a bitch, but tell us why the valedictorian needs the S.A.T. answers."

"I'm not the valedictorian," Anna argued. "I'm second."

"Oh." Francesca could make a word as short as "Oh" drip with sarcasm. "Well, that explains it."

"Everyone has their reasons for being here,"

I said. "We don't need to know them."

"I think we do," Francesca insisted. "It'll be like that scene in *The Breakfast Club*, where they all get high and make confessions to one another."

"Sweet!" Roy perked up at the word "high."

"Maybe we should," Matty said. Then he saw straight-arrow Desmond and added, "Maybe we should all say why we're here."

Anna looked at me. "You said we wouldn't have to." She was so clearly worried. I could have hugged her right then and there.

"Me first," Francesca said. "I'm here to make new friends. And for the wine, of course."

"How 'bout you, superstar?" Matty asked Desmond. I still didn't think we should go down this road, but it looked like we were too far now to turn back.

Desmond sized Matty up and said, "I'm here because the S.A.T. is racist."

"Well, that didn't take long," Matty replied under his breath.

This pissed Desmond off. "Oh," he said, "and you don't think it is? Who created the test? Rich white guys. Who do you suppose scores highest on it?"

"Asian chicks," Roy put in.

We all looked at him.

"Middle-class Asian girls who watch less

than an hour of television a day," Roy explained.

Where did he get that from?

Matty snorted. Desmond glared at him.

"What about you?" Desmond asked. "Why are you here?"

"Because I'm not smart enough to get the score I need," Matty said, all casual. "As opposed to being a genius who's being screwed by the man."

"Matty," I warned. I wasn't going to have any of that. Best friend or no.

"But it is, you know," Anna spoke up. "Unfair to certain groups."

"Like kiss-ass valedictorians?" Francesca asked.

She's not valedictorian, I thought.

"I'm not valedictorian," Anna said.

Francesca clearly didn't care. "Oh, right. You're second."

This was getting us nowhere. If not backward.

"Enough," I said. "Now, I'm sorry we're in the coat room here, but this isn't a joke." I uncovered the blueprints. "These are the floor plans for the tower that houses the regional ETS offices." I held up a binder. "This is the hardware schedule that tells us the specs of the security cameras that are here, here, and here."

Roy stuck his nose in his wineglass and inhaled. "Fruity," he said. "And yet woodsy."

"Pay attention, Roy," I told him. I felt like a goddamn schoolteacher. And this was going to be a real screwed-up field trip. We had to focus. "Francesca has the codes to the locks inside ETS," I continued. "And we know where the test answers are filed. So if you think—"

Just then, Desmond's cell phone rang.

And he answered it.

Good-bye, focus.

"Yeah," he said to whomever had called, and began to chat.

Roy leaned over and examined Larry's bedspread, wondering aloud if it was made of hemp.

Matty turned to me and said, "This'll never work."

"We'll be all right," I told Matty.

He didn't look convinced. "Yeah," he said with a sigh. "We'll be great. All State's phone ringing off the hook, Roy trying to smoke Larry's comforter."

I swiveled to see Roy ready to light the whole thing up.

"You're about out of here," I warned him.

Roy shrugged, then looked at Francesca, who was wrestling with her laptop.

"Need some help?" Roy asked.

"Not unless you can code visual basic," Francesca replied, her voice making it clear that such a thing was about as likely as her going out with him.

Roy just took it. He leaned over to her and shifted her from the keyboard. Then he typed in a rapid series of commands, capped with a triumphant hit of the return key. Francesca looked somewhere between terrified and amazed.

"What'd you do?" she asked.

"Some stuff with dynamic variables," Roy replied.

It was a night of surprises, I tell you. Before I could say anything, Desmond had loudly wrapped up his call.

"So we gonna do this or what?" he joked.

Matty didn't think it was funny. "Yeah, we're gonna do this," he said. "So how 'bout you hang up the phone and pay attention."

Matty looked to me. "You better get your boy straight," he warned.

"You got a problem with me?" Desmond shot back.

"I got a problem with anyone who puts us at risk," Matty answered hotly.

"And you think that's me. Man, I don't need this grief," Desmond announced, then started for the door.

He turned to Anna and asked her if she was down with this.

Anna looked to me for an answer, her eyes pleading for a resolution.

I had to think fast.

I had to keep in mind everything we wanted. What we were here for. We were forgetting that.

"You guys see Desmond last weekend on TV?" I asked.

The strangeness of the question got their attention. We all knew Desmond hadn't been on TV. And yet . . .

"Playing for St. John's?" I continued. "He took twenty-five and ten off North Carolina."

They still didn't get it.

"Matty," I said, turning to him. "You saw the game, right? You and Sandy were in your apartment at Maryland."

A year from now. If we make this happen.

Anna clued in. "I didn't see it," she volunteered. "I had a date. But my roommate at Brown is a big sports fan, and she said it was pretty great."

"It was," I said. "I saw the whole thing from my dorm room at Cornell."

If only. If only.

Roy still looked confused.

"You had money on it," I told him.

Finally, he got it.

"I hope you covered the spread," he muttered to Desmond.

"We can do this," I said to them all. "We can all get where we want to go. But we need to trust one another."

Desmond held his ground at the door. "You talk a good game," he said, "but I half expect your mom to pop in with snacks. This is serious. Some of us have a lot to lose."

"We all have a lot to lose," Matty pointed out.

"Fair enough," I said. "Just hear me out. Anyone who doesn't like the plan can walk."

And I had them. They were all with me.

But would that last?

(28)
Kyle

I placed a thumbtack on the ETS blueprint and began to tell them what I'd worked out.

"Friday afternoon, Francesca will enter through the lobby," I began. "The same as any other Friday. Then she'll make separate appointments for me and Matty with her dad's firm."

Nobody would question her. I had faith that she wouldn't let them.

"What if he recognizes you?" Roy asked.

I knew he was talking about the guard, not Francesca's father.

"He won't recognize me," I assured them.

"He might," Roy said.

I imagined the guard pushing a security button. SWAT teams pouring into the lobby as sirens wailed. Guns drawn, the SWAT captain yelling at me to get down. . . .

"He won't recognize me," I said again. I moved Matty's and my pins onto the blueprint. "Once I'm up, Matty will sign in and join us in Francesca's father's office. The three of us will stay there until after hours."

"Where am I going to be?" Roy asked. Suddenly so interested.

"You're waiting in the woods nearby," I said, trying to remain patient.

"With that big ass crow? Alone?"

We're breaking and entering, and he's worried about a crow?

I told him he'd be with Desmond and Anna. Roy got this crazy look on his face then. Like he was imagining doing something besides crowing with Anna.

Anna looked a little sick at the thought. "Maybe we should all go together," she said.

"We need you outside on the perimeter for when the night guard makes his rounds," I explained. I held up some of her photos to show the guard's surveillance. "Their rotation isn't very precise, and we'll be using flashlights inside."

"So we'll watch for the guard to tell you when to douse them," Desmond said, getting it.

"That's right," I replied. The flashlights would be way too easy to spot in the darkness.

We needed to be sure the guard was nowhere around when we used them.

I put three thumbtacks on the outskirts of ETS to show where Roy, Anna, and Desmond would be.

"Inside," I continued, "Francesca will ask the night security guard to disconnect the alarm on the rear stairwell door, claiming she has some boxes to unload from her car—something she's done in the past.

"Meanwhile, Matty and I will have about twenty seconds to get inside the stairwell before the guard returns to the front desk and his security bank of monitors.

"We take the stairs to the roof and wait for Francesca's key card," I said.

"What about the alarm on the roof door?" Desmond asked. I noticed I had his full attention now. You could see his mind was working the same way it did on the court—trying to find holes in the opposition.

"It's disabled because the employees go up there to smoke," Francesca explained.

"That's right," Roy added.

We all looked at him. How did he know?

"What?" he went on. "I lost you guys last time, so I went up for a little puff."

Whatever. Hopefully he'd be nowhere near the roof this time around.

I pointed to the rooftop and pressed on.

"From here, we're almost home," I said. "We get in, we get the answers, and we get out." All we'd need to do was use a rope ladder to go down through ETS's skylight.

I held up the pushpin that I'd used to track my movements. "Shortly after midnight, this is me," I said, moving the pin to the safety of the woods outside the building. "Twenty-five minutes into Saturday morning, and a whole lot closer to the rest of my life."

I scanned the room. They seemed inspired.

"Who's gonna join me?" I asked.

Matty, God bless him, was first, moving his pushpin next to mine. Francesca was next. Then Roy. Anna looked at Desmond, then moved her pin to be with ours. After a beat, Desmond joined us.

The plans of six became one.

(29)
Matty

It was a lot to think about.

It was a lot to believe in.

If it had been anyone else but Kyle, I would have been out of there. If it had been any girl besides Sandy waiting for me, I wouldn't have even considered it.

Suddenly Larry's place was too loud—not the place I wanted to be. I went out for some air. I'd seen Francesca go out there. I followed. Lingered.

She was smoking. For some reason I was surprised by this. I imagined her having bigger secrets than that.

"You smoke," I said.

She just shot me a glance, then looked away. Leaning in the darkness.

"It makes kissing kinda nasty," I pointed out.

"We won't be kissing," she pointed right back.

"I know," I said. "It's just . . ."

It was just what? Even I didn't know how that sentence was going to end. So I left it alone.

Francesca blew a few smoke rings—she was really good at it—and then asked, "Why are you here, Matty?"

"I don't know. It's a nice night."

"No. Why are you involved with this?"

I thought that was obvious. "I need the answers," I said.

"To join Sandy at Maryland," she mimicked, mocking me. "But what's so great about her? I mean, aside from being smoke-free."

How could I explain? "You won't get it," I said.

"Try me," Francesca replied.

So I did. I tried. And it was easier than I thought it would be. All I had to do was think of Sandy and all these words came out of me.

"I had a thing for her since freshman year," I told Francesca. "It took me until junior year to ask her out, and after that things were better, you know? It's like, I don't get the best grades and I'm not great at anything, like Rhodes is

All-World and Kyle's so talented. Roy's got dope." Francesca smiled. She knew what I meant.

"But here was something I was finally great at," I continued. "I was great at being with Sandy. I could make her laugh and guess what she was thinking and it was all . . . great. It was all great."

"And?" Francesca said.

I looked at her right in the eye. Probably the first time I ever did that.

"And I can't wait to be great again."

I couldn't let go of it.

I would miss it too much.

(30)
Kyle

The last few days before the exam passed like most days. More or less.

We all felt like we were carrying around this big secret. Some of us had dealt with our own big secrets before—me with the truth about my S.A.T. score, for example. But this time was different. This time the secret was shared.

We didn't talk about it in school. But we acknowledged it in other ways. We acknowledged that we were a team.

Desmond sent a fast wink to Roy in the halls. Giving the ghost his due.

Roy liked that.

Francesca was snagged by a security guard for being late to school. But Anna bailed her out, sliding over her camera bag and pretending that Francesca had been helping her with yearbook photos. Vice Principal Merrell wasn't about to question Anna Ross, Star Pupil. So Francesca was off the hook.

And Matty. Well, Matty was still thinking of Sandy. But he didn't freak out when Francesca plastered a skater girl sticker over one of Sandy's photos in his locker.

I felt more confident. I felt like we were together for a reason. Walking the halls was like running downhill. The feeling of momentum.

Then it stopped.

It was time.

I went to Matty's house the night before. He was on the roof, as always. Watching the neighbor again.

"When do you think it changed for him?" Matty asked me. "I mean from living life to just watching it on TV?"

"Maybe he's just playing the cards he was dealt," I said.

Matty took a good look at me. That best-friend look.

"You having second thoughts?" he asked.

"It's real, Matt," I told him. "Tomorrow it's all real. And if we get caught, that's real too. For Dez and Francesca and Anna—"

"Roy," Matty put in.

"And you," I said.

We stepped to the edge of the roof.

"This one's on me," Matty said quietly. "I don't know how many times you've said that after bailing me out of something. And I appreciate it, Kyle. I do. But I came to this on my own. We all did. We all need it now."

This was why I loved Matty. The coming out and saying it. That thing between us.

I looked at the neighbor. My attention swam through his television light, his dim room.

"If you could be anything you wanted to be, and money was no object, what would you be?" I asked.

"Porn star," he joked. Then he got serious. "Nah, I don't know. Just happy, I guess. You?"

"Architect."

"Architect or Cornell Architect?" Matty asked, knowing me too well.

"Cornell Architect," I answered, more sure of that than of anything else.

"Well, I hate to say it, but last I checked, you can't get there from here."

I nodded. Getting to Cornell required a leap.

And we were about to take it.

31
Matty

We all prepared in different ways. Roy became obsessed with the heist in the movie *Heat*. Kyle read those blueprints like he was an evangelist studying the Bible. And I kept psyching myself up. Sometimes I said the usual thing, Sandy, Sandy, Sandy. And sometimes I caught myself shaking it up a little.

Kyle, Francesca, Kyle, Francesca, Anna, Desmond, Roy, Kyle, Francesca.

Francesca did her job and got Kyle and me on the appointment list. I watched from the car as Kyle signed in. No problem. But that didn't make it any easier. It wouldn't be the first time Kyle succeeded at something while I fell flat on my face. I was yelling at myself to keep cool, which is never an effective way to keep cool. I got up to the guard and expected him to just laugh at me, to tell me to get lost. But, much to my surprise, he waved me in. I headed straight to the elevators before he could change his mind.

I made my way to Francesca's father's office. It was your usual office, nicely decorated. I couldn't see a picture of Francesca anywhere, but maybe she'd removed them.

We didn't rest for a moment. We didn't think about how far we'd gotten. All we could think about was how far we had left to go.

Kyle called Desmond to make sure the phone contact was working.

"Hey, it's me," he said. "Set your phone to vibrate and call me back." Desmond did, without a hitch.

"All right," Kyle said. (Man, I was glad he was in charge.) "We'll use redial from now on. Tell Roy to do the same."

When Kyle hung up, he said, "He wished us good luck."

I wasn't just wishing. I was praying.

Francesca left to work her magic on the night guard. As she did, Kyle and I made a mad dash down the halls, getting to the stairwell before the guard returned to the monitors.

The stairwell was dark, but Francesca's expression when she arrived wasn't. Maybe I was too nervous to see that she was nervous. But from where I stood, she looked real cool.

She swiped her key card, and the light went green.

Easy as that.

We headed up to the roof. I fought the temptation to look for Desmond, Anna, and Roy below us. I fought the temptation to scream from all the tension I was feeling.

We made it to the skylight, and Kyle looked worried.

"The skylight's locked," he said.

That was it. It was over.

"Just kidding." He smiled.

I swear to God, if he wasn't my best friend, I would've pushed him right through the sky-light, glass and all.

Francesca and I unspooled the rope ladder from the box she'd carried up. The night guard hadn't even asked her what was in it—he knew better than to mess with the boss's daughter. We dangled it down to the top floor. Our bridge to the future.

"Masks," Kyle instructed. We'd decided it was better that they couldn't see our faces if by chance we showed up on the security cameras.

Francesca pulled out a bloody stump to wear. Kyle slipped on the face of a buck-toothed hillbilly. And I . . . well, I took out the only thing I could get in a hurry.

"Going snorkeling, Matty?" Kyle teased.

"It's all I could find," I mumbled before putting on the swim mask and puckering up to the snorkel.

Together we descended into ETS. We were going down into a conference room. Once we were all there, Kyle took out the blueprint and turned on his flashlight.

This was going to be the most dangerous part. The real breaking in.

Kyle traced our route with the beam of light. "Leave the masks on until we're past the security cameras," he warned us. "Just in case."

Then we were off. I could vaguely see Kyle walk through the conference room door. I tried to follow, but rammed right into the door frame.

"Walk much?" Francesca asked.

"My mask is fogged," I explained.

Quickly I wiped it off.

It fogged up again.

There wasn't any time to do anything about it. Kyle had a timetable and he wasn't waiting. I caught up to him, and the three of us made it through the corridors. Kyle had forged a cheat sheet from the blueprints that he could consult while stealing the S.A.T. How fitting.

"There's a security camera around this corner

to the right," he told us. "It has a red light on top that lights when it detects motion. Stay low and stick to the wall."

"What'll we do if it sees us?" Francesca asked.

"'Bout three to six months and a ton of community service," Kyle replied.

Jail humor. Real funny.

My mask was getting foggier and foggier. It was like a big ass cloud had settled in the hallway.

Kyle dropped out of my sight. It took me a second to realize he was only following his own advice: stay low and stick to the wall. I wasn't so blinded that I couldn't see how short Francesca's skirt was—not bad for crawling behind.

"Ladies first," I said.

"Well, get going, then," she shot back.

Ouch.

I thought I could do the stop-drop-and-roll thing. But I was breathing harder now, and that fogged me up even more.

"Matt, you okay?" Kyle called out.

"I can't see through the mask," I admitted.

"Just head forward," Francesca offered. "Two o'clock."

Two o'clock? I was supposed to be telling time now?

"C'mon, Matty," Francesca said, suddenly serious. "Trust me."

She held out her hand. I took it.

"Thanks," I said.

We'd made it past the cameras. We rose and took off our masks. I expected Francesca to make a comment, to ridicule my foolishness in some way. But she just looked at me like she cared. It was so strange.

Kyle was back with his cheat sheet. "This way," he said.

Francesca and I followed him forward. Through the maze of cubicles. Off to slay the dragon.

(32)
Roy

I was the wild ghost dog patrolling the jungle. I was the hunter stalking the great black crow. I was the stranger in the moonlit woods. I was—

"Your turn to watch for the guard, Roy," Desmond broke in. "You got your phone set?"

I checked my celestial navigation. I checked my place in the universe. I checked my grandest devices.

"I got it," I said.

I stepped to the edge of the woods. They were spooky, and I was spooked.

Time for another joint.

I pulled my arrow from my quiver. I prepared the antidote. I—

"Can I ask you a question?" Anna said,

which was in itself a question. "Why do you smoke pot?"

I rolled on. "Something to do," I said. "Why do you bite your fingernails?"

Anna's finger was just about at her face. Then she shoved her hands hard into her pocket. Denying herself.

I would not do the same.

I was the watchman in the tower. I was the bugler about to make the call. I was the wolf in the clearing.

I was really spooked.

(33)
Kyle

Office 510.

The place where S.A.T. answer sheets went to be filed.

"This is it," I said. "Francesca."

That was her cue. She took out the master security code list, checked it with the help of her flashlight, then punched in the code.

Turning the knob, she said, "Ladies and gentlemen, I give you . . ."

An empty room.

". . . a serious waste of time," Francesca concluded.

The room wasn't just empty. It was desolate. Abandoned.

"Why would you lock the door to this?" Matty asked.

"This was it," I insisted. "I swear it. The answers went to 510 for filing." That was what Arnie Branch had said.

I couldn't believe it.

"Yeah, well, 'went to' doesn't help us, does it, stud?" Francesca wasn't exactly hiding her disappointment.

I felt mine was going to crush me at any moment.

"Stress And Tension," Matty said. "S.A.T."

"Sandy's A Transvestite," Francesca added. "FYI."

I trailed into the room and scanned the emptiness. The total emptiness. As empty as my future.

I went to the window and looked out onto the city. It was as distant to me now as any chances I'd ever had.

"I should've known I couldn't do this," I admitted.

Man, it hurt.

"C'mon, Kyle," Matty said, trying to help. "You didn't know."

No comfort. It was great that he was trying to give it, but I just couldn't take it.

"Nah," I said dismissively. "I screwed it up. I had those answers right in my hands."

Then I remembered the look on that guy's face and what he'd said when he handed them over.

Great, he had said. *I need three copies of this on rush. One comes back to me. One goes to Anne Clark. And the master goes to 510 for filing. Got it?*

The master goes to 510 . . . and—

"One comes back to me," I said aloud.

That was it.

One more chance.

I darted away. I had to find Arnie Branch's office again. He had to have printed the answers out again. Had to have given them to another copy guy. Had to have gotten his one copy back.

"Kyle—," Matty called out to me.

Suddenly a sharp white light flooded in from the hall. The door to ETS was being opened.

We weren't alone.

I froze, then spun around to shield Francesca, blocking her right before she was going to come out in the open, into the light. Matty rammed into her from behind, but I put my hand over his mouth before he could protest our sandwichlike state.

We remained in our hushed, motionless huddle as a flashlight beam pierced the darkness, cutting through the office in a bright line. It was like one of those prison movies, when the escaping convicts stand against the wall as the searchlights try to flood them out. This light was clearly looking for intruders. And we were intruders.

I was afraid to breathe. Afraid to move.

One more sweep of the light. And then, mercifully, it began to retreat. The flashlight bearer headed back out the door, closing it again, returning the office to shadows.

After another scared moment, Francesca wriggled free of our extended embrace.

"Ew," she said.

"Who the hell was that?" I asked. The night guard wasn't supposed to make his rounds for a few more minutes.

"That was Bernie, the Creepy Lobby Guard Who Hits on Everyone," Francesca explained. Clearly she was not a fan.

I checked my watch to make sure I hadn't lost track of time (along with everything else).

"He's early," I observed.

Time was a luxury we didn't have anymore. We had to keep moving.

"Kyle," Matty said quietly, still a little rattled by our almost-capture, "where are we going?"

I led them back to the conference room and said it again.

"One comes back to me."

They didn't get it. I explained: "The guy who sent me to copy the answers. He said, 'The master goes to 510 and one comes back to me.'"

"So what?" Francesca said sourly. "You wanna call him at home?"

"I wanna find his office," I said. "545."

I looked down to the master blueprint.

There it was.

(34) Anna

My first stakeout!

Okay, it wasn't exactly what I'd thought it would be. Roy was off in his own purple haze, and Desmond wasn't in a talkative mood. But that didn't matter as I wandered off a little. I headed into the woods and stared for a while at the moon. I didn't even need to take a photograph—I knew I would remember this moment. I wasn't thinking about college or clubs or even exams. I was just full of the present, and the present was enough.

I looked over to see Roy trying to leap up to a tree branch. Maybe he wanted to swing from branch to branch like Tarzan. But at this rate, he'd never make it. I turned my eyes back to the ETS building.

A guard. I saw a guard—heading straight for Kyle, Francesca, and Matty!

Quickly I ran to Roy. This was our moment.

"Roy," I said. "The guard."

For some reason, Roy was standing in the stream. "There's a problem with my phone," he said.

"What problem?"

He held up a dripping wet, moss-covered phone. That explained the stream. Like Roy, the phone was useless now.

I darted back to the car. I couldn't run fast enough.

Dez looked at me like I was crazy.

"Phone!" I cried.

He tossed his phone to me. I fumbled for the redial.

Kyle answered!

"Yeah," he said, having no idea.

"Shutoffthelightsshutoffthelights," I ordered.

I saw their flashlights going off.

Just in time.

We waited to see what the guard would do. He paused, looked around a little. Then moved away from Kyle's direction.

Whew.

Roy grabbed the phone and sheepishly dialed them up.

"Sorry," he said. "All clear."

Kyle said something, then Roy hung up.

"Matty says he's kicking my ass," Roy reported.

I think it was clear that neither Dez nor I could blame him. We quickly relieved Roy of his lookout duties, and he went back to tackling that tree branch.

My heart was still racing from all the excitement. I guess I had known all the risks involved, but this was the first time I'd really felt it. And it made me . . . a little giddy.

Once Dez and I had settled in, eyes not leaving the building, I asked him, "What's it like when the crowd cheers for you?" Was it as exciting as what we were doing now?

"You never played sports?" Desmond asked. Like such a thing never ever happened in America.

"Nah," I said, freak as usual. "I've never done anything, really. Except this."

Dez accepted that. "Sometimes it's like it's not even me," he confided. "It's like it's magic."

"Yeah," I agreed. "I forget to believe in magic sometimes. I study and study and I worry that one of these days I'm going to study it all away. Until there's no room for it."

It's like your life just falls one way.

Unless you push it in another direction.

Matty

I know Kyle was the Master of the Blueprints, but I was the one who found the office first.

"I got it," I said, all happy. "Office 545."

Francesca scanned her list of security codes and gave us the right one.

I would like to say that we treated Mr. Branch's office with total respect and courtesy. But, hell, we were in a rush, so we just tore through it, looking for the answers.

It wasn't in any of the files.

It wasn't in his in box or his out box.

It wasn't in any of the stacks of books or under any of the paperweights.

Screwed Again There.

Then I spied his computer.

"Maybe it's in here," I said, sitting down in

front of it. I loaded up, only to be asked for a password.

Stuck And Tormented.

"You know what this means?" Kyle asked. He didn't look too good.

Francesca, Kyle, and I all looked at one another.

We needed the last person we wanted to need.

Kyle wasn't taking any chances. He called Desmond's phone and asked for Roy.

"Roy," he said. "We need your help." He was spooked.

I could hear Roy on the other end.

"It's Kyle, Roy."

After about another minute of back and forth, followed by ten seconds of telling Desmond what we needed, we retreated to Plan B. Or, more accurately, we made up Plan B on the spot.

"You're going to need a diversion," Francesca pointed out.

Roy was the only one of us who had a chance of hacking into the computer before we were collecting social security. And to do that, we needed to take Bernie the Smarmy Guard's attention away from the monitors.

A minute later I was calling Dave at Clyde's Mini-Market.

"Dave," I said, trying to keep my voice down just in case Bernie decided to make another tour of the floor. "It's Matty."

"Hey, Matty. Don't tell me you're running low on the Bull already."

Oh man, I could've used a Bull right then. But I tried not to let that distract me.

"Nah," I said. "I need some flowers delivered."

"Roses," Francesca said from my side.

"Make it roses," I told Dave. "And . . . you think you could hook me up with a bottle of champagne?" (A cheap one, I hoped.)

"Yeah," Dave said. "I could do that."

That's what so great about mini-market employees. They're like bartenders—they don't ask too many questions.

"Sweet," I said. "And could you sign a card? Um . . . 'from your secret admirer.'" It was very *Brady Bunch*, but I figured it would work. I mean, there was no way that Bernie was smarter than Jan. I gave Bernie's name and address to Dave.

"All right, man," he said. "'Bout half an hour for delivery, huh? Oh, and dude—good luck with Bernie."

D'oh d'oh d'oh.

"Thanks," I said. What else could I say?

After I hung up, Francesca just asked,

"Well?" When I told her what Dave had said about Bernie, she snorted out a chuckle.

"I told you you should've called." Not pleased.

"Shh. So what do we do now?" she asked.

We looked to Kyle. This was his game.

"I guess we wait," he said. "Up top."

(36)
Roy

Think of it as an S.A.T. problem, I said to myself.

"The black guy, the pothead, and the brain get stuck in the spooky-ass forest . . . ," I started. Out loud.

We were headed closer to the enemy fortress.

"I think it's nice," the brain said. "Like an adventure."

But Dorothy, I don't think we're in Kansas anymore.

When we got to the edge of the woods, we stopped for a moment. And Dorothy asked me, "If you could do anything with your life and money was no object, what would you do?"

I thought about it for a second. Anything at all?

"When I was a kid, I used to play this video game for hours," I said. "Street Fighter 2. I remember thinking people get paid to do this. Ya know, think up the game and create the characters. Like there's this one street fighter, Blanka. He's like a half-lizard, half-human that eats his opponents. I mean, he either zaps them with lightning or he bites their faces with his fangs. Pretty cool, huh?"

"So you'd design video games," Dorothy said.

"Nah," I told her. "I'd kinda like to be Blanka."

Ready to rumble.

(37)
Francesca

We were on top of the roof, waiting for Matty's Mini-Market Minion to arrive when Matty asked me, out of the blue, "If you could do anything with your life and money was no object, what would you do?"

What kind of wrong question was that? Money was always an object. And you could never do just anything with your life.

After giving me a moment, Matty said, "Francesca won't answer. She'd actually have to share something real with us."

"Yeah," I said, "and what was your answer, Matty?"

"Porn star."

Oh, that was something real to share.

"See," I said. "You took mine."

"But I was joking," he replied, almost gently. "I'd probably be an actor, I guess."

"As opposed to, say, solving world hunger or curing a terminal disease."

He wouldn't look at me. Just said, "See what I mean?" to Kyle.

Okay, fine. I didn't have to be the bitch in this scenario. He wanted to share, I could share.

"Maybe I'd run a no-kill animal shelter," I told him. "Or send free stretch limos to all the city bus stops. Or maybe I'd be a mom. Not just a mother, but an actual mom who cared more about the title of parent than the one on her business card."

Silence.

C'mon, boys. Don't leave me hanging here.

"Or porn," I added. We were getting too serious.

A pair of headlights cut through the night, just like our flashlights had cut through the dark office.

Delivery time.

(38)
Anna

From the bushes, we saw the delivery car arrive.

"This is us," Dez said.

My heart just kept beating faster and faster. I suddenly understood that phrase—a rush. It was a rush. My mind was a rush, my heart was a rush, and the whole moment was a rush. Even when we were standing still.

Roy stretched, like he was getting ready for a track meet. I wondered if I should stretch too. I knew I was supposed to stay still. But what if Roy needed us? What if we all had to make it inside?

"All right, Roy," Dez coached. "When Francesca opens that door, you haul ass."

"What do we do?" I asked. Guard his back? Clear his path? Jump the guard?

"You're gonna wait here with me," Dez told me. "They just need Roy."

I knew that. Really, I knew that.

But couldn't they need us, too?

"You ready, flash?" Dez asked Roy.

He seemed a little winded to me. Then he hacked a cough the size of Minnesota.

"You gotta get off the bong, Roy," Dez said.

I could see the delivery guy knocking on the front door, a bottle and bouquet in his hands. By now, Francesca would be waiting at the bottom of the stairwell, ready to open the back door the minute the guard was distracted. Matty and Kyle would be waiting on the roof.

And I would be waiting . . . here. For the rest of the night.

Roy started to wobble a little more. Even in his sprinter's stance.

"You're sure they just need Roy?" I asked Dez. "Maybe we should go too."

"Just Roy, Anna," Dez warned.

The guard opened the door for the delivery man. Francesca scooted out the back door and waved us in.

Us. Okay, maybe it wasn't us. Maybe it was just Roy. When I saw her wave, it was like an invitation. I had to accept it. I had to be a part of this. I had waited on the outside my whole life while other people had fun and took action. This was my turn. The door was open.

I ran.

39

Desmond

"Aw, hell no," I muttered.

But it was too late. Anna makin' like she was doing the hundred-yard dash. Roy trailing behind her in his mess of a way. And me. What the hell was I supposed to do? I knew what teams were about. I knew that sometimes you had to put yourself on the line in order to get the win. And I sure knew that I wasn't going to be waiting in the woods all night alone.

So I made it in, right there behind them.

Which isn't to say I wasn't brewing mad.

"What the hell was that?" I blasted at Anna.

Francesca was on the phone with Kyle. As we started up the stairs, she said, "He's in. Plus two."

Anna was right at her heels. Practically flying.

Roy was another matter. Panting like a dying horse.

"Aw, man," he cried. "Not steps!"

We could hear the delivery car drive away as we hit the roof. Matty helped lower us down through the skylight.

Kyle was waiting there. Looking at me like I was a parent who couldn't make his kids behave in the supermarket.

"What happened, Dez?" he asked. "We just wanted Roy."

"Tell that to Marion Jones, there," I said, motioning to Anna.

Kyle gave her a look, and suddenly Warrior Woman was turning her volume down a few notches.

"I guess I misunderstood," she said. "Sorry."

"Well, there's no going back now," Kyle said, forgiving her real easy. "Everyone stay close. C'mon."

And I thought to myself, *Yeah, there is definitely no going back now.* And maybe no going forward, either. I'll admit—when I was running to the building, I was thinking about Anna, and even about Roy. But now, as we walked through this silent office building, nothing more than righteous thieves, I started to think about myself. About how many college teams would want a kid with an arrest record. About the headlines they'd make out of this. I'd be a bigger story than I'd ever been. Not because of my talent or my skill. No—for my utter stupidity. He threw it all away, they'd say. And then they'd move on to someone else they wanted. I knew that. I'd known that all along.

We made it to the office.

"We think the answers are on this computer, Roy," Kyle said.

"There's a password."

Roy picked up a photo from the desk. "This the guy?" he asked.

Kyle nodded, and Roy studied the picture closely. All I saw was a grinning office man. No passwords there.

Roy typed in a password.

No go.

Another.

Nothing.

Then he eyed the photo again and typed.

A beep.

I looked at the screen.

We were in.

Roy shook his head at the guy's photo. "You're a filthy man, Arnie," he said. Then he turned to Kyle and asked, "What'd they call this thing?"

"Verification Master," Kyle told him.

Roy typed in the search.

Nothing. Then there it was.

"'Mercer County S.A.T. Exam,'" Kyle read out. "Print it and let's go."

Easy as a layup.

We all watched as Roy hit "print." Then the S.A.T. made a half-count jumper to win the game.

"You need three other passwords from three other people in order to print it," Roy said.

"You think you can figure it out?" I asked.

"Sure," he said. "Just gimme six months and the CIA mainframe."

It's like we all just crashed at once.

"Whelp," Francesca said, "this was fun."

But Kyle wasn't giving up.

"Guys," he said, "the exam's right here."

"Yeah," Francesca snarked. "Throw in the answers and ya got me."

And Kyle said, "Exactly."

A man with a plan.

40

Kyle

We had gotten this far. We weren't stupid. But it wasn't going to be an easy sell.

"Guys, the questions are right here," I said. "Now maybe we thought this thing was bigger than us one on one, but no way it beats all six of us together."

Matty started to find some lame excuse, but I cut him off.

"Just try this," I said, and then read from the computer screen.

"'If it takes fifteen people eight hours to make one hundred items, how many hours would it take six people, working at the same rate, to make half as many items?'"

Silence.

"Dude," Roy said. "That's, like . . . impossible."

"No, c'mon," I insisted. "Think. Francesca."

We could do this. I knew we could do this. We had to.

"Well, it depends," Francesca responded. "Is it these six people? Because if it is, is 'infinity' one of the answers?"

This was what the S.A.T. had done to us. We knew it was unfair. We knew it tested us on things that didn't really matter. We knew the scores weren't an accurate reflection of who we were. And yet, we'd let it beat us up. We'd taken our failures to heart. Secretly we thought the test knew something about us that we were trying to deny—that we weren't smart. That everything else was a fake and the test was the only thing real. I looked at Anna and Matty and Desmond and Francesca and even Roy—they all had their strengths. But right now, all the S.A.T. could do was make them think of their weaknesses.

Was there any way around this? Was I strong enough to do it alone?

No. I wasn't.

But then Anna said, "Ten. It's ten hours."

I eyed the test on the screen. That was one of the options.

"B," I said. "Ten."

One answer. That's what it took. The possibility of one right answer.

Francesca leaned over to the screen and read, "'A ten-quart mixture consists by volume of one part juice to nine parts water—'"

"Jesus, what lightweight's mixing this drink?" Roy interrupted.

Francesca went on. "'If x quarts of juice and y quarts of water are added to this mixture to make a twenty-seven quart mixture that consists by volume of one part juice to two parts water, what is the value of x?'"

All eyes turned to Anna. She had the kind of expression that you could tell meant she was doing the equation in her head. It was damn cute.

"Nine?" she answered less than positively.

All eyes turned to Francesca.

"Well . . . C is nine."

Another one down.

But then Desmond said, "Eight."

Anna still disagreed, and gave her reasoning.

"We already have nine parts water (y), and nine goes into twenty-seven three times. So for a one-to-two ratio, you'd have eighteen parts water (y), and nine parts juice (x)."

"So it's nine," Matty said.

"They said if x quarts of juice are added, what is the value of x," Desmond pointed out.

"We started with one part juice. So nine minus one equals x."

"Eight?" Roy looked to Francesca to check the screen.

She smiled. "D. Eight."

Impressive. Very impressive. And so beyond my scope.

But I had other talents and they could help on other questions.

"That's two down. Guys, we can walk away right now, but what are we walking back to? I say we trust one another's talents and take a shot as a group."

Matty always had my back when it counted. "He's right. We can do this," he said.

"Unless we run out of time," Francesca pointed out. Pessimist to the end.

"So we'll divide it up," I suggested. Roy punched up the test on another terminal in the office, and we were set.

"Done. How 'bout it, Francesca? You wanna take a crack at the verbal?"

"Nah," Francesca declined. "Me and words . . . not so goodly."

"All right," I decided. "Anna and I can do the verbal. But someone's gotta do the math."

"I'll do it," Desmond volunteered.

"You sure?" I asked. "I mean, it might be kind of—"

He cut me off. "You ever heard the term 'stereotype justification?'" he asked. Then he glanced at Anna and winked. "Math doesn't scare me," he continued. "You just take care of the verbal."

"Okay," I said. "Who's helping Dez?"

Roy shrugged, then said, "I guess I can. But only with quadratic equations, coordinate geometry, and algebraic visualization. If you want."

Show-off.

Roy bolted from the room, on fire now. Dez shook his head and followed.

"It looks like me and you, Hasselhoff," Francesca said. "We'll watch the lobby."

So now Anna and I were alone.

"Is this why you asked me to come?" she said.

"No," I told her. "I thought we'd get the answers." This option hadn't crossed my mind.

"Then why'd you include me?" she asked.

And I thought—the answer is right now. The way she looked. The vulnerability and the strength mixed together. The fear and the daring.

But how could I tell her that? Instead I deflected.

"Why'd you tank your first exam?" I asked, bringing us back to out-of-bounds.

She looked away, and I felt bad. I backed off.

"Let's just do this," I said.

The rest might follow.

(41)
Matty

So there we were, staking out the lobby. Protecting the test-takers. Keeping one another company.

Or not.

Francesca wasn't talking to me. She just painted her fingernails with Wite-Out. I was left to my own tangents, which as usual led me to Sandy. Her painting her nails while I looked on.

"You know," I said, "Sandy liked this blue color. Trueberry Blue."

"But not anymore," Francesca replied, still focused on her own nails.

I didn't follow. How would Francesca know if Sandy switched nail color?

Francesca looked up at me. "You said liked. Sandy liked."

"Likes," I corrected. Was it such a big deal?

Francesca nodded, then looked hard at me. I almost had to turn away. Nobody usually saw me like that.

"She doesn't call anymore," she said. Like she already knew it was a fact.

"She calls," I told her.

"Not like before."

Now, how did she know this? I mean, yes, Sandy had a lot to do at school. Busier now. But the only person I'd told was—

"What'd Kyle tell you?" I asked.

"Nothing. You just told me."

"She's busy," I explained. Like I'd been explaining to myself.

"You won't get her back, Matt," Francesca said. She wasn't making fun of me or anything. She said it like she cared. "Or the way it was. You won't get that back with her."

"You don't know anything about it," I lashed out. Her words hurt.

"I know it's not healthy."

"Right," I said. "And folding yourself into a Web page because Daddy doesn't love you enough is."

Oh Jesus. Why did I say that? She'd hurt me, and I was fool enough to want to hurt her back. I regretted it as soon as I was done.

"I'm sorry," I said. "I didn't mean that."

And now she was trying to hide it. I was going to throw my hurt at her, and she was going to wallpaper over hers with a grin.

"Then why'd you say it?" she asked.

"Because she doesn't call anymore," I admitted.

After a quiet second together, she spoke. "You said you were great at being Sandy's boyfriend. But you weren't."

"That's nice, Francesca," I said. "Rub it in."

Then she leaned in and kissed me. Just like that.

What are kisses about? With Sandy, it was about keeping in touch. About establishing what we had.

But this kiss—it was different. It was about the hurt. It was about the moment. It was about being lost in the dark.

It was there, and then it was over. She retreated to the exit.

"You weren't great at being some girl's boyfriend, Matty," she told me. "You just found someone who let you be okay with yourself."

When she was gone, the kiss lingered.

And so did her words.

(42)
Desmond

I was used to playing under pressure, playing against the clock.

Roy was not.

"X is to y—," I began.

"—as this crap is to boring," Roy concluded.

I decided to ignore him. There were a lot of questions to get through.

"What score do you need on the test, anyway?" Roy asked.

I told him 900.

"And *you're* taking the math for us?" Roy was very amused.

"I was afraid of the verbal, Roy," I explained. "I could ace the math and still not get a 900. Without that, I'm Prop 16."

"How's that work?"

This was one question I could answer easily.

"I can't play or practice in college for a year. Last time I did that I was five."

"So why not go pro?"

Another easy question.

"You don't know my mom," I told him. "She's all about the college degree. But she works three jobs. If I blow out a knee in college or my game falls apart, you know what I got? Credits. If I go pro this year and I blow out a knee, you know what I got? Five years guaranteed at more than a million per."

"What's she say when you tell her that?"

"I don't. I can't. You don't know my mom."

Roy nodded, then asked, "All this because you can't talk to your mom?"

That was about it.

"Can you talk to yours?" I challenged.

"My mom's dead," he replied, like it was no big deal. "But if she wasn't? Yeah. I think I could talk to her."

I took in what he said. It made sense in a way. And what I said must've gotten to him a little too, 'cause all of a sudden he was off his ass and on his game.

"All right, lemme in there," he said.

Roy shoved me away from the screen and

started typing. As long as he was answering questions, I threw him a couple more.

"So what do you need the answers for, Roy? Black market cash?"

"Slippery Rock University," he said.

I couldn't believe it.

"Slippery Rock University?"

He nodded. He wasn't just saying this.

"It made *Playboy's* top party schools, 1987."

"You know," Roy said, "a lot of people think these questions are difficult, but not me."

"No?" I wanted to hear more.

"Nah. These questions all have answers."

I thought about it for a minute. Then we both headed back to the test. The one of many tests.

(43)
Kyle

When I allowed myself to take a break from the verbal—when I allowed my mind to wander just a little—I wondered if what we were doing wasn't a better preparation for life than any S.A.T. would be. Combining forces. Working together. Finding people with different knowledges to figure things out.

Made sense to me.

Desmond and Roy returned just as Anna and I were checking over our half. Francesca came by to see what was happening, leaving Matty on lookout.

"We good?" I asked.

Desmond nodded.

We were set.

It was unbelievable.

"Let's get out of here," I said.

We headed back to the conference room and met up with Matty, ready to climb back to the roof. Roy went first. But he couldn't get himself up. His bag was too heavy.

"Roy?" I said. "What the hell's in your backpack?"

"Nothing," he replied, like a four-year-old snagged with pudding from the fridge.

We did not need this. Over Roy's protests, Desmond and I dumped out the bag. It was full of office supplies.

"I needed some school supplies," Roy insisted.

"You can't take this stuff," I told him.

"Why not?" Roy challenged petulantly.

"Because if anything's missing, Francesca will be a suspect," Matty pointed out.

"So?"

Oh, man. I pulled someone's framed family photo from the bag.

"Why the hell did you take someone's family portrait?" I asked, trying to stop myself from getting too mad.

"The wife's hot," Roy answered. Desmond led him away to return the goods.

"C'mon, dog," Dez said. "I'll help you put it back." Francesca and Matty said they'd go too.

That left me and Anna. We climbed up to

the roof and sat near the skylight. I checked my watch. The city would be waking up soon.

In any other circumstance, this would have been ideal. On top of the world, watching the sunrise. A girl I liked beside me. A girl who maybe could like me back.

Anna began to pace the rooftop. Happy.

"I can't believe it," she said. "This is so awesome."

I had to smile back. "You got your answers," I said.

"Well yeah, that too . . . but . . . all of it. We did it."

Anna let out a whoop, forgetting where she was. I reminded her.

"Shh," I urged. "We haven't done anything yet. What's going on with you, anyway?"

" I don't know," she said, still giddy. "I guess I'm having fun."

She crossed over to me and sat close.

"I mean, I know how those people see me. Like you know those girls that are perfect, the ones everything always works out for. I always wanted to punch one of them in the mouth."

I had to grin at that.

"I'm not a robot," Anna continued. "I just haven't done that much, yet."

"Well, if it helps," I offered, "there's a lot of stuff I haven't done too."

"Yeah, but I've really never done anything. Like break curfew or cut class or . . . make out on a rooftop."

The sky was day now. The look she gave me was a little like blind faith, somewhat like fading summer, and definitely like a moment of clarity.

It was beautiful.

I was about to kiss her. She was about to kiss me.

But then the office lights flickered in the skylight beneath us.

The workday had begun.

And we were caught in it.

(44)
Matty

As soon as we heard the footsteps and the lights started going on, we darted back to the conference room.

"What happened?" Kyle asked from the roof.

"Someone's here," I told him.

We all rushed for the rope ladder—and it broke underneath us.

Not good.

Kyle gripped a pipe on the roof and leaned in.

"Grab my arm and we'll pull you up," he said.

"Francesca first," I said. But when I turned for her, she wasn't there.

She was gone.

Roy, Desmond, and I looked around. Then Desmond spied something.

Francesca. Hiding beneath a cubicle desktop. Cut off. No way to escape.

Looking scared.

"What's wrong?" Kyle called out.

Just then, Francesca's key card slid under the conference room door. She was giving it to us. Giving herself up.

"Francesca's not gonna make it," I said.

A shadow grew on the corridor wall. Footsteps closer.

I knew what I had to do.

"We gotta go," I said. I picked up the key card.

Desmond sneered. "Man, that's just wrong," he said. "We're not leaving her here."

I saw her through the glass.

I knew what I had to do.

"We don't have a choice," I insisted. "Now let's go."

"No way," he dug in.

"I'll go," Roy volunteered.

"Rhodes," I said, trying to talk as tall as I could. "If your ass doesn't get through that skylight, the rest of us are screwed. Francesca knew the risks, and so did you."

"He's right, Dez," Kyle said, backing me.

"This is messed up," Desmond said. But he

took the key card, and he leaped his way to the roof. Then he swiveled to help lift Roy. Roy jumped . . . and missed Desmond's hand.

"You gotta get off the bong, Roy," Desmond chided him.

"I know it," Roy conceded.

Roy jumped again and made it this time.

That left me.

"Matty," Kyle called.

I saw his outstretched hand. I was sure we'd make it. But then I saw Francesca. And all her tough-girl shell was gone. She was just as frightened as the rest of us.

I knew what I had to do.

"I'm good," I told Kyle.

"What?" He didn't get it.

"I'm good, Kyle," I repeated. I tossed Roy's stupid backpack through the skylight. Then I took a computer from a work station in the corner of the room.

"Matt," Kyle said, in that way that he says it. The call to sanity. The plea for rationality.

Not this time.

"What about Sandy?" he pleaded.

"What about her?" I replied.

He looked at me. He got it now.

He had to let me go.

"This one's on me," I told him.

The guard was almost here. I made eye

contact with Francesca—and flipped her off. She wouldn't have it any other way. Then I picked up the computer and stepped right into Bernie's path.

"Freeze it," he demanded.

I froze it. I gave him my best caught-in-the-act act.

He'd gotten his criminal.

The rest would go free.

(45)
Kyle

If I hadn't been on the roof, I would've stopped him. I would've joined him. I would've been able to do something besides leave.

I knew Anna, Desmond, and Roy didn't know the way like I did. I knew that what Matty was doing was something that he, in his own twisted way, wanted to do.

"I gotta go back," I said, once I'd led the rest of them to the back stairway.

"Kyle," Desmond said, gently but firmly. "It's done. You can't help it. The rest of us need you, man."

He was right. And it felt so wrong.

I'd liked being in charge. Now it felt like the worst burden in the world.

"We'll use the key card and go out the back

160

door," I instructed, barely there. "Desmond and Roy go right, we'll go left. We'll meet at the exam in the morning. I'll bring copies."

We got to the bottom. We got to the door. We walked out into the daylight.

It should've felt great.

It felt awful.

(46) Roy

Tired. I felt so tired. All this stuff—breaking into buildings, fending off crows, caring about other people—it takes a lot of energy.

Desmond drove me home in his posh ride. When we got to my house, he said, "Your pops gonna come down on you for being out all night?"

"Nah," I said. "My dad died with my mom. Not for real, but . . . for the most part."

Desmond looked at me hard. Hard, but caringlike. He said, "You know the test seemed like a breeze for you, Roy. Why'd you do this?"

"I don't know," I said. "I guess I just wanted to hang out."

I popped open the door before Dez could say anything else. I decided to leave him with this: the fact that there were a lot of high school hoops stars who didn't make it in the Big Time right out of high school. He just wasn't ready yet.

No shame in that.

I crept quietly into the house and headed to the place I most wanted to be.

Couch sweet couch.

Bong sweet bong.

PlayStation sweet PlayStation.

Home sweet home.

Desmond

I took the ball to the net. I couldn't sleep now, so I went outside. I remembered how long Mom had to save to get this house, this driveway, this net. I took shot after shot. I made most of them. Missed some. But the important thing was that it didn't matter as much. Don't get me wrong— it still mattered. But it wasn't everything.

Mom got home from her late shift. She saw me and sat down on the bench by our net. I stopped playing and came over to her. Her eyes met mine, and I realized how much she knew me, and how I had to have faith in that.

I knew I couldn't tell her what I'd been up to that night.

But in that moment I knew I could tell her everything else.

(48)
Kyle

It would have been simple to say I wanted to undo it all. I probably would have, if I could've gotten Matty back. But in my heart I knew the Matty part was the only thing I wanted to undo. Matty and I started this whole thing feeling we were alone on a dead end. Now we had Anna and Francesca and Desmond and Roy. We had the knowledge that we could do something. And we had our own answers to the test that had plagued us.

I'd gotten so much out of it. But if I lost Matty, none of it would be worth it.

After Anna dropped me off, I trudged to my house. I discovered Larry sitting on the steps, guitar in hand.

"How'd it go?" he asked.

"Don't you sleep?" I asked back. I didn't want to deal with him right then. I just wanted to close my door and break down.

"What happened to you, Kyle?" Larry called after me.

I turned back. "What happened to me? What happened to you? You were my big brother."

"And what—now I'm the walking dead?"

I was too exhausted. Physically and mentally exhausted. I couldn't dance around this right now.

"Pretty much," I told him. "I mean—how do you think Mom and Dad feel?"

"How do you think they feel?"

"I don't know, Larry. Not good, probably."

"Well," Larry said, "if you were a parent, which would you prefer? The son who lives above the garage, or the son who cheated his way into college."

Great. He knew.

I was surprised how little I cared. I mean, hit me again.

"Matty got arrested," I informed my dear brother.

"You think it was an even trade?" he asked, relentless.

"I think that's a crummy thing to ask," I told him.

"Well, at least now you sound like my brother. Maybe he's actually in there somewhere."

I slumped onto the steps.

Just what Matty thought, I figured.

"Anything you don't know, Larry?" I asked.

"I'll tell you something you don't know," he said. He was enjoying this. "Every Christmas after you go to bed, Dad and Mom and I sit up and talk about how proud we are of you. How great it is to be around someone who has his whole life in front of him and genuinely deserves it because he's a good kid who does the right thing."

I think this was the most generous thing my brother had said to me since I was five. I almost couldn't take it.

"Every Christmas for how long?" I asked.

"I don't know." Larry shrugged. "Ten years or so."

"And you didn't think I'd like to sit up with my family on Christmas?"

"You'd just stress us out."

Okay. Time to end this conversation while it was still in the plus column. I got up, ready to head in.

"Word of advice?" Larry offered.

"Why not?" I said.

"Never take advice from anyone who lives above a garage."

Words to take to heart.

I got back to my room and sat at my drafting table. I picked up one of the log cabins I'd made of Popsicle sticks. Back when I was little. Back when life was easier. Back before tests.

Outside, I could hear Larry playing his guitar. My first instinct was to close the window. But then I saw Larry and I realized my first instinct was wrong. I opened the window a little wider. He was giving me music, and I would accept it.

Then I did what I always did when I was stressed, when life was too overwhelming.

I drew.

And this time, I drew something that mattered.

Anna.

(49)
Roy

So I woke up on the couch, reached for my bong, and found it in Desmond's mom's hands.

Talk about waking up on the wrong side of the couch.

I closed my eyes, counted to three, opened them again. This time I saw Desmond there too.

"How long since your mother passed, baby?" Desmond's mom said.

"About nine years ago," I told her. "I was seven."

This big black mom woman just nodded in the middle of my PlayStation den. "That's a shame," she went on. "My son tells me you encouraged him to talk to me. You're a smart boy, Roy. Why you doing a stupid thing like drugs?"

This was like a total ambush. I couldn't even take a toke to help me out.

"Something to do?" I answered. Clearly there was no use lying to this woman.

She nodded again. "Something to do. Mm-hmm. Volunteer work is something to do. Respecting yourself is something to do. Making your mother proud."

I nodded to that.

She continued. "You know how they say, thank the Lord my mother's not alive to see this? Well, somebody's mother is. And I'm not happy with this, Roy."

"I'm sorry?" I sputtered.

WHO WAS THIS CRAZY WOMAN?!

"You get yourself a shower and some clean clothes," she ordered. "We'll wait. Fix you some breakfast before your exam."

I sat up and forced a smile. "I've been thinking about that, Mrs. . . ." I couldn't remember her last name ". . . Desmond's Mom. I'm not taking that exam. I mean, let's face it, I'm not going to college. And even if I did, I'd just be taking a seat from someone who wanted to be there more than me."

Desmond's mom shot Desmond a look. I could tell I'd been a popular topic of conversation that morning.

"You are a smart boy, Roy," Mother of

Desmond told me. "But, baby, there's a whole lot of dumb dribbling out of your mouth right now."

She was angry now. The persuasive kind of angry.

"Now, did you hear what I said about the shower and clothes?" she commanded.

"Yes, ma'am," I found myself replying.

"You'll find I don't like to repeat myself."

Dude, I could've figured that out on my own.

"Yes, ma'am," I repeated.

She shot me a look.

So I said it again. And then I bolted for the shower.

It was out of my hands, I tell you.

Resistance was futile.

(50)

Francesca

When I got home, I thought for a moment about knocking on my father's door, trying to find something there.

But that moment passed. And so did my stay at home. I had somewhere I had to be. With cash.

It took me awhile to find the county jail, and then it took me a little longer to pay the bail.

My mind was still replaying the scene on a loop—Matty coming out with that stupid computer in his hands. Bernie doing the whole police routine on him. The cops coming. Me hiding out in my father's office. Safe. Because of Matty.

The fool.

He looked a little worse for wear coming out of his cell. And I could tell he was a little surprised that I was the one there. But not totally surprised. And neither was I.

"I gotta tell ya," I said as he got close, "not everyone can pull it off—but the dashing criminal thing looks pretty good on you."

"Wait'll you smell it," he replied.

He came up to me and shuffled a little. Poor guy. He had no clue how I felt.

He had no clue that I definitely had a clue.

"You know," he said, "I was thinking in there. I need to work on being alone."

I nodded. And then I kissed him, hard and deep.

"Or not," he peeped.

He threw his arm around me as we walked away from the jail.

"Anyone ever tell you you're a helluva kisser?" he said. (I didn't tell him yes.) "Not as good as my cellmate, Ramon. But not bad."

"What about the exam?" I asked.

"Here's the thing. Once you've spent the night in jail with the worst versions of who you could be someday, the S.A.T. ain't nothing."

We got to my car. "How 'bout you?" he continued. "You all right?"

I nodded. And it was true. I was all right.

All right with me.

All right with him.

"Yeah," I said. "It's gonna be a nice day."

We climbed into the car. Suddenly I didn't want any distance between us. I leaned over and gave him a peck, which turned into a bite of the lip.

"Sick And Twisted," he said. "S.A.T."

"Yeah," I agreed. "Secretly A Tease."

I started the engine. He smiled at me, and that's all that mattered.

"Something About Trust," he concluded.

Yeah. Something about trust.

(51)
Anna

So much had happened. Just as my heart had raced before, my mind was racing now. I returned to my parents' morning routine. Mom exercising. Dad playing the news junkie. But this time everything was different.

Because I was different.

Mom and Daddy exchanged alarmed looks when I stumbled in—sleepless and wide awake. Their little girl, out all night.

I didn't know what to say to them.

And then I realized: I didn't have to say anything.

I just poured myself a cup of coffee, grabbed a bagel, and headed to my room.

I had an S.A.T. to prepare for, after all.

o o o

When it was time to drive to school, my mother had found her voice again.

"It's unacceptable, Anna," she said. "You're out all night doing God knows what, with God knows whom, jeopardizing everything we've worked for on the eve of the biggest day of your life. This is the real world, honey. You feel pressured? You deal with it. You don't stay out all night. This is your last chance to get into Brown."

Suddenly the words came.

"Oh, that reminds me," I told my mom, "I'm not going to Brown."

She was speechless. And I felt the need to add, "Now you deal with it."

No more pressure.

Just life.

(52)
Kyle

I did my share. I copied the answers onto cheat sheets for everyone.

But nobody wanted them.

Anna arrived first. Looking *really* good and striking a confident pose.

"Wow," I said. "Check you out."

"Yeah," Anna said, clearly pleased. "I just told my mom I'm not going to Brown."

I couldn't help but observe that the boys at Brown were gonna be disappointed.

"So if not Brown, then where are you going?" I asked. Somehow I felt my own future was tied to the answer.

"I don't know," she said. "Europe, maybe. Then college."

"Sounds like a plan," I replied.

I was so proud of her.

Roy and Desmond were next up, surprising me by arriving together. I offered them the cheat sheets.

"Nah," Desmond said. "I already nailed the math. Plus, you don't know my mom."

"Really?" I said. "Roy?"

He shook his head. "Shit, you don't know D's mom."

Finally Matty and Francesca arrived. I was not surprised that they were together. Matty looked a little beat up. But he also looked happy. I imagined she had something to do with that.

I tried to find the words to say to Matty all I needed to say to him, but with a single look, he waved them off. He knew it all without it needing to be said. He knew I loved him before and I loved him now. He knew that our friendship would continue to face all sorts of crazy things, and we'd keep paying each other back, over and over and over again.

Desmond pulled him into an embrace. "I wanted to go back for you, but Kyle said screw y'all."

Thanks, Dez.

Francesca stepped over and gave Anna a full stare.

"You look like a slut," she said. Then she grinned. "I like it."

"Thanks," Anna said. "You too."

Now I got my chance to speak.

"You okay?" I asked Matty quietly.

"Yeah," he said. "I mean, on the one hand, I got arrested. But on the other, my old man won't hire anyone with a criminal record."

He smiled. I tried to return it. But it still hurt me, everything that had happened.

"I'm sorry, Matt," I told him.

"Don't be. Besides, it's not all that bad." He gestured to Francesca, and that said it all.

I offered him one of the cheat sheets.

"Keep it," he said. "I don't need it now."

"C'mon, man," I protested. "Stop it."

"I'm serious."

I knew he was, but he'd gone through so much for them. He deserved them the most.

"Take the answers, Matty," I insisted.

"Nope," he insisted back.

"Matt, you got arrested."

"I don't need 'em."

"Take 'em."

But he wasn't going to.

"Unbelievable," I said. "Here, Francesca." I offered them to her.

"Nah," she told me.

"What is this?" I asked.

"What?" Francesca answered. "I was never in it for the answers. I got a 1460 last semester."

"You didn't tell us that!" I exclaimed. I couldn't believe it. Or maybe I could.

"You didn't ask," Francesca pointed out.

I turned to Anna.

"How about you, Not-Going-to-Brown Girl?"

"Do I look like I need the answers?" she replied.

"You look like you need a pimp," Roy cracked.

Anna ignored it.

"I'm the valedictorian," she proclaimed.

"You're second," Desmond reminded her.

"For now." She smiled.

I looked around, then back at my hand. I was still holding the cheat sheets.

"Hold up," I said. "Are you telling me that, after all this, nobody's using these answers?"

"You are," Matty answered. "Aren't you?"

And then I realized: I wasn't going to use them either.

"No," I said.

"Why not?" Matty asked, still looking out for me.

"Because my brother's an asshole," I told him. "And because it's not me."

"Kyle, it's your dream, man," Matty tried again.

I told him it was. But if they wanted to put a number on that, then screw 'em.

I know who I am.

"Yeah?" Matty asked. "And when did you have this moment of clarity?"

"About the time my jackass best friend got arrested," I told him.

He grinned at that.

"So all this was for nothing?" Matty asked.

I looked around the group. All of us, together.

"If you call this 'nothing,'" I replied.

They all nodded.

We all knew it was something. Friends. Allies. Something good.

"Man, screw this," Roy said. He snatched the cheat sheets from my hand and darted for the door.

I didn't miss them. At all.

I held open the door. Anna smiled and walked in. I needed one more moment. To look at the day. To feel the possibilities.

To let go.

To hold on.

(53)
Kyle

That morning I saw the future. I saw my life the way I wanted it to be. And it was different from before.

Roy didn't cheat. But there was no way he was gonna let all that work go to waste.

Let's just say there are five stoners with near-perfect S.A.T. scores attending very prestigious universities because of a certain break-in.

Desmond owned up to his desire to turn pro, and his mother respected him. But the hard truth was that he wasn't yet first-round material.

So he withdrew his name from the draft and enrolled at St. John's.

Last weekend on TV, I watched him take twenty-five and ten off North Carolina.

The day after the S.A.T., Francesca shut down her Web site. She told me she'd thought of a better way to fight injustice.

She's aiming now for law school. I figure our phones are going to ring about the time she takes the bar exam.

Matty survived probation and some serious community service.

I asked him once what he would be if he could be anything at all. He said he might like to be an actor, or maybe he'd just try to be happy.

Now, with Francesca at his side, he's trying for them both.

Roy scored alarmingly well on the exam. But that didn't exactly offset his 0.0 GPA.

Eventually, he was guided to his GED . . . under Desmond's mom's watchful gaze.

These days he still spends most of his time on video games. As a matter of fact, last year, eight of the ten best-selling games were created by him.

I retook the test and did okay. Anna crushed me. When it came time for college, she said no to Brown and opted for Penn. Her parents survived it. I'm at Syracuse.

One of these days some of the greatest architects of our time will come from Syracuse, New York. And, anyway, we had an idea. . . .

Something that mattered to someone.

Now every other weekend, when a woman boards a train at midnight and, three hours later, a man joins her, we now know what happens.

Life happens. Romance. A little adventure.

The stuff you won't find on a test.

Because, you see, you can test us all you want. And use the results to project our potential. But what number do you put on heart? How do you grade determination? Where's the pass/fail line for dreams? The proficiency curve for courage? Or the baseline for desire?

Where's the equation that interprets that instinctual feeling that you can do better, and the personal drive that compels you to try?

Before you answer, you should know it's a trick question. There are either many answers or none at all. But do your best and pick one.

And keep in mind—you will be graded.

❀ WANTED ❀

Single Teen Reader in search of a FUN romantic comedy read!

How Not to Spend Your Senior Year
BY CAMERON DOKEY

Royally Jacked
BY NICOLE BURNHAM

How I Spent My Last Night on Earth
BY TODD STRASSER

From E to You
BY CHRIS D'LACEY AND LINDA NEWBERY

Mates, Dates, and . . .
BY CATHY HOPKINS

Ripped at the Seams
BY NANCY KRULIK

★ *Available from Simon Pulse* ★
✳ *Published by Simon & Schuster* ✳

♥ ❀ ♥ ❀ ♥ ❀ ♥ ❀ ♥ ❀ ♥ ❀